Many people helped me to make this
the best book I could possibly write.
Many thanks goes to K.G., my editor, for all her hard work.
To Rachelle Fox for her expert guitar advice.
To my teen readers, Glen and Denise.

Published in 2007 by Simply Read Books Inc.
www.simplyreadbooks.com

Text © 2007 by James McCann
Cover and interior images © 2007 by A. Matsoureff

Book Design by Jacqueline Wang

Library and Archives Canada Cataloguing in Publication
McCann, J. Alfred (James Alfred)
Pyre / James McCann.

ISBN 978-1-894965-66-8

I. Title.

PS8575.C387P97 2007   jC813'.54   C2007-902032-1

Printed in Canada   10 9 8 7 6 5 4 3 2 1

We gratefully acknowledge the support of the Canada Council for the Arts
and the BC Arts Council for our publishing program.

James McCann

Pyre

SIMPLY READ BOOKS

Contents

PROLOGUE
OCTOBER 17TH, 1989. SATURDAY.

"Hey, Mr. Conway, time to close up!" Mike shouted from the cash register at the front of the store. He waited for a response, then locked the front door and flipped the *OPEN* sign to *CLOSED*. From where he stood he could see the doorway to the back room.

When Mr. Conway didn't respond, Mike looked at his watch: 9:05 p.m. He still had two hours of homework to do. Should he just walk out? He would, except that working for Conway was his community service project. He had to do it, no matter what it took.

"Mr. Conway," Mike shouted as he walked towards the back room. He could hear snoring even before he opened the curtain that separated the front and back. Three hours ago Mr. Conway had said he was going to unpack stock, but there he lay, sprawled on top of unopened boxes, fast asleep.

"Which one of us is the adult?" Mike whispered, shaking his boss awake.

"Oh! Mike! I must have dozed off for a minute. Why don't you help me unpack the new stock?"

Mike sighed. "We're closed, Mr. Conway. Seriously. It's almost ten after nine."

A look of confusion washed over his boss's face. He

blushed as he said, "Trina kept me up late last night. You know how pregnant women are."

Not really. But I do know how drunks are, Mike thought, pretending not to notice the half-empty bottle of whiskey on the floor. "Why don't I close up tonight?" Mike said aloud. "Think you can stay awake long enough to make it home across the street?"

Mr. Conway laughed. "You're a good boy, Mike. If I have a son, I hope he turns out as good as you."

"See you Saturday, Mr. Conway."

Mike locked the back door behind Mr. Conway before returning to the cash register. He never felt so alone as he did in Conway Groceries when it was so quiet that he could hear the clock ticking and the wind beating against the windows. He thought back to a time when the night was filled with excitement and adventure. A small part of him missed that life, even though that's what got him this community service.

A rap on the front door startled Mike. He looked up.

Behind the glass door stood a stocky teenage boy, clad in a black leather jacket and dark sunglasses. His long black hair blew in the wind.

"Sorry, we're closed!" shouted Mike.

"I just need a few things. Only five minutes," the boy called out.

I'm never going to get home, Mike thought. He considered ignoring the stranger and closing up, but the point of this job was to learn how to put the needs of others before his own. He opened the door and the stranger rushed past him, accompanied by a gust of cold air.

"Do you know what you need?"

The stranger stood with his back to him. His shoulders rose and fell with an even rhythm. His hands were at his side, palms open.

"You were adopted three years ago by the Nevervilles. Is that true?"

Mike leaned against the counter. "Yes. Do you know them?"

The stranger sighed. It sounded like a growl. "I know what you are, Mike."

Mike smiled. He stood a few inches shorter than the stranger, and he was certainly not as muscular. "Maybe you should take off."

"You aren't afraid of me?"

"If you know what I am, then you know why."

The stranger slowly turned to face the teen. He removed his shades, revealing startling emerald eyes. "Do you know what I am?"

"Look, buddy, I'm giving you one chance to get out." Mike opened the front door.

The stranger smiled. Then he threw open his jacket and drew two short graphite stakes holstered to his chest.

"Holy crap, you're a hunter!" Mike cried. He turned and grabbed the door but was stopped by the stranger yanking him back by his shirt. Mike punched him repeatedly in the face until he was loose. Once free, he ran out the door into the cold outside.

Fresh wet snow covered the ground, but Mike managed to keep his footing. He cut across streets and yards towards the graveyard to the north. The sun had set hours ago, and the snow glowed beneath the full moon. Mike fled up a hill crest, then into a dip where tombstones marked those who had once lived in the town.

He looked behind him and saw nothing but the fallen snow. He crouched behind a large tombstone, the wind whispering as it blew snowflakes through the air. It made him feel trapped, as if he were imprisoned within a snow globe.

Suddenly, the bay of a wolf echoed over the graveyard.

Mike closed his eyes and bit his lower lip. He couldn't stop his hands from shaking, and every time he drew a breath it rasped in his throat. He knew the only way to live would be to run, to flee from the graveyard and hide. But where could he go?

"Mike!" he heard the stranger yell.

Mike considered staying put. What if he hid there until sunrise? Would someone come for him? When would his parents come looking for him? When would they call the police? *And if they do come, will the hunter kill them to get to me?* He stood. His legs buckled beneath him and he had to catch his balance by grabbing the tombstone. The stranger, holding a stake in each hand, stood on the other side.

"Why are you doing this?" Mike said through broken sobs.

The stranger walked around the stone, until he stared Mike directly in the eyes. "To release you from a life you never chose." The stranger drove a stake through Mike's chest, filling the silence with the cries of a boy carried by the howl of a wolf.

November 6, 1998.

Before the vampyres came, I thought they were all evil. Actually, I thought they were all make-believe. Now I know differently. Not only do they exist, but there are those who wish to do good in this world. What I don't know is how to tell the good ones from the bad.

I've been a Defender for just over ten years, and I know I've killed more than my share of the good ones thinking they were evil. Believe me when I say I've done a world of good by doing what I do.

This deal I've made, to protect the good vamps, is not wholly one-sided. They get to see another sunset, while I get a place to play my music. Chances are if you've ever been to the youth raves or underage clubs you've probably heard me. But you haven't seen me. I hide behind my music where people don't notice me. You hear the music, but you never see the musician. That's a part of survival.

In high school, I tried to live the same way. But it's harder to live under the radar when bullies are determined to boost their reputation by beating you up. I suppose I'm not that much different from them now.

CHAPTER ONE

OCTOBER 24TH, 1989. TUESDAY.

"I t's time we sent this bastard a message," Nick said, handing Jon a can of red spray-paint.

Jon sat on the floor of Nick's van, propped up against the back seat staring out a side window. The van was a typical prairie ride, a rusted white exterior masking its cheesy plush velvet interior.

The sun, which had yet to set fully, glistened across the barren horizon. A few street lamps flickered as the world prepared for darkness. A light sheen of fresh snow had fallen, the kind that would only stay through the night. Nick had parked across from the local community center, the After Dusk, an unkempt bungalow surrounded by a lawn as high as the first floor windows. The center looked abandoned, with boarded-up windows, chipped paint and shingles that rattled with every gust of wind.

Jon, Bob, Trevor, and, of course, Nick sat inside the van. Nick, the crew's leader, said when to jump, how high to jump and where to jump. He was the biggest of all the seniors at Fillmore High. His sandy hair hung loose over his shoulders but was cut tight at the sides. Icy blue eyes and a bright white smile made him look like a natural helmsman for a Viking ship.

But this being the twentieth century, Nick was reduced

to waging wars on anyone who didn't fit in with his gang. Tonight he had chosen Saint Whittaker, the guy who ran the After Dusk, as his target. Whittaker had come to Minitaw three years ago with Mike. After pairing Mike successfully with the Nevervilles, he had begun a crusade of finding homes for orphaned teens. Rumor had it that Nick had tried forcing Mike onto his Lunch Money Collection Program, without success.

Trevor slid the side door open and Jon stepped out. He was wearing black sweats, a long sleeve sweater and a knit hat. Earlier the outfit had made him feel like James Bond, but now it made him feel like a geek. *What am I doing?* he asked himself, watching Nick climb out to stand beside him. *Right. Not getting beat up.*

"Okay, nerd." Nick grabbed Jon by the collar and glared deep into his eyes. "You have one shot at this. Screw it up, and it's my fist in your face. Got it?"

"Dude, I got it. Seriously."

Nick let him go. "Just remember to keep your eyes to yourself. You look at Karen after this and I won't offer you a way to work off the debt."

Jon gripped the can of spray paint to stop his hand from shaking. It didn't work. A knot crunched in his stomach as he walked around the van. The last trace of sun shrank from sight, just as the moon rose and the stars opened.

Nick climbed into the driver's seat and gave Jon a mean look. He pointed to the bungalow, and Jon reminded himself of their pact: tag "GET OUT OF MINITAW" on the house and they'd be even. "For now," Nick had added. All this for looking at Karen Burrard at lunch. *It was still worth it,* thought Jon.

Although it took only a few seconds to cross the road, it felt like a lifetime. He dropped to his knees and, hidden by the grass, crept towards the house. The cold air nipped his ears, but Jon preferred its bite to Nick's fists.

Halfway across the lawn Jon noticed something odd. A bluish fog circled around the house only as deep as the grass. The fog didn't pour out into the street. It was contained to the grass, as if it were a part of the lawn itself.

A horn blasted. Jon turned and looked up over the grass to see Nick laugh, then mimic a fist hitting his palm. Nick pointed at the bungalow, his face now dark and serious. Jon continued crawling until he crouched next to the house.

As Jon lifted the can, the fog followed his actions. He lowered the can and the fog retreated. "This is too weird," Jon whispered. He turned and saw Nick again pound a fist into an open palm. Message received.

Breathe, he told himself. *I won't get caught. I won't get caught.* He shook the can and lifted it high. Pressing the nozzle, he began the first stroke. As quickly as the paint left the can, the fog caught it. The red liquid ran off the fog and hit the grass beneath. Not a drop stained the house.

"What the hell?" Jon blinked. As his eyes closed and opened, the fog disappeared, and a bony hand grabbed his shoulder.

Nick's van squealed away, the sound of burning rubber piercing Jon's ears. He turned to face Saint Whittaker. Tall and lanky, Saint Whittaker was dressed in a gray pin-striped suit and fedora hat. He looked more like a 1920s gangster than a youth social worker.

Jon didn't know what to say. He wasn't sure that he had the power to say or do anything except stare at the old man. He didn't even drop the spray can. Whittaker looked Jon up and down before removing Jon's knit hat. Jon's long hair fell over his face, and, when he brushed it aside, Whittaker handed him back the hat.

"What a friendly town this is! You've come to paint the community center?"

"Huh?" Jon muttered.

Saint Whittaker let Jon go and then stepped back from the bungalow. "But I don't like red. What do you say you come back tomorrow evening, stay for dinner, and after that you can tend the lawn before you paint. You can paint over the weekend."

"Whoa, wait a sec." Jon stood up. The old man still towered over him. Jon hated being so scrawny. "I'm really sorry about this but . . ."

"But what? Are you going to tell me that you came here to vandalize the town's only teen community center? I was so hoping not to have to call your parents."

"C'mon, man. You don't have to call my parents." Jon now understood the saying "between a rock and a hard place."

"Do your parents know where you are?"

"They never notice when I'm gone," Jon mumbled. Then, only slightly louder, he added, "How about I come tomorrow after school, and Saturday afternoon?"

"Tomorrow, Thursday and all day Saturday," Saint Whittaker corrected.

Jon sighed. "I have to work on Thursday, and I can't do

this all day Saturday. How about tomorrow, Friday and late Saturday afternoon?"

Whittaker smiled and patted Jon's back. "So nice of you to volunteer!"

"Whatever, dude. But once the grass is cut and the house is painted we're even, right?"

Whittaker kept smiling. Before turning to the After Dusk he said, "I never make promises. I never make promises."

When the door shut and Jon was alone in the grass, the chill returned. He started back toward his home but stopped to look at the bungalow. He'd passed it dozens of times without ever thinking about it, but now it was one more thing that made his life in Minitaw miserable.

CHAPTER TWO
OCTOBER 25TH, 1989. WEDNESDAY.

osmo barked once before leaping onto Jon's stomach. Sitting bolt upright, Jon instinctively grabbed his dog's mouth before sneaking a peak at the alarm. *6:00 a.m.* He listened for a few seconds to make sure his dad hadn't woken up.

Jon didn't understand how his mutt knew when it was 6:00 a.m. every morning, but at least he'd never sleep in if the alarm failed. As Jon scratched Cosmo's ear, the dog cocked his head and got a glossy look in his eyes. Jon had learned to keep this moment short. After all, the dog had not woken him up for attention.

"Need to go outside?" Jon said in a voice most people reserved for small children.

The dog perked and jumped from the bed. Jon groaned as one of Cosmo's hind legs landed on his bladder.

"Rowf!" Cosmo barked, sensing his master's hesitation.

"Shh! You'll get us both in trouble!" Jon got up and ran down the stairs, nearly tripping over Cosmo, who had taken the rush as a race. Jon rounded the corner at the bottom, laughing. Before darting for the rear door, Cosmo leaped in a circle and pushed Jon to the ground.

"Some people don't have to get up this early!" his dad yelled from his bedroom.

"Sorry," Jon muttered, walking into the kitchen. He could hear his mom arguing to keep his dad from coming downstairs. Quickly, Jon slipped into his runners, grabbed his jacket and headed out the door.

No one woke up this early in Minitaw. Families stayed tucked into their warm beds, in their homes with their perfectly-raked lawns and white picket fences. Last night's snowfall had melted with the sunrise, leaving behind a glistening sheen on the town's brown grass. The trees, having lost their leaves weeks ago, resembled rows of wooden skeletons. The look fit the time of year, as everyone prepared for Halloween. Pumpkins carved into demonic expressions guarded doorsteps, cardboard cutouts of witches hung in windows, and fake spider webs covered porches.

Jon didn't care much for Halloween. As a teenager, the end of October marked Fillmore High's first big dance. This year the dance committee called it "Halloween Dreams," and made it a Sadie Hawkins dance, which meant the girls had to ask the guys out. To Jon this meant two things: first, he'd have to suffer the humiliation of not getting asked and, second, he'd have to pretend not to care.

Cosmo sniffed and marked every tree on the block while Jon began to think about his horrible deal with Saint Whittaker. What was stopping the coot from turning him in after he had the After Dark painted? And who would believe Whittaker anyway, without a shred of evidence?

Jon called Cosmo to go back home. As he did, he knew the whole town would believe the man who single-handedly paired loving couples with teen adoptees over him. More than anyone else, his mom and dad would believe Whittaker. And Jon had disappointed his macho father enough. As for Mom, the last thing he wanted was to hear that "sigh" or get that "look."

His parents still weren't up, so Jon snuck upstairs to the bathroom. He closed the door, keeping Cosmo outside in the hallway. His dog lay against the door, pushing his body up against it as if guarding the entryway. That amused Jon.

Although a German Shepherd, Cosmo was only a year old and would sooner lick a perpetrator to death before he'd bite one. Jon remembered the time Lea, his neighbor and best friend, had strolled into the yard, unaware of the new addition to the Pyre family. Jon had gone inside to phone her when Cosmo laid his two beady eyes on the intruder. He let out a low growl, Lea screamed, Cosmo yelped and both scurried behind trees for safety.

That had made her laugh, and picking up his ball, she coaxed Cosmo out. When Jon returned to the backyard, he'd found the two of them playing together like the best of friends. *Maybe Lea will ask me to the dance . . . it's not like she's in with the cool kids.*

Jon stared at the mirror, which was not his favorite thing in the house. Every time he looked in it, he was reminded of his pale complexion, sallow cheeks and shapeless arms. He'd grown his black hair long like Stevie Ray Vaughan, but other than his hair he looked nothing like his idol.

With plenty of time to spare before first period, Jon left with his backpack and guitar. It was a Yamaha C-40 that he'd found at a garage sale six years ago. It wasn't as cool as the 1962 Sunburst Fender Stratocaster Stevie Ray Vaughan played, but it was cheap and had a sweet sound.

He always picked up Lea, although lately she took longer and longer to get ready. He knocked at the front door and her mom answered, still attired in a bathrobe. She was the kind of single mom that made all the married ladies in the town nervous. Tall, fit and curvy, Ms. Black always put the emphasis on "Ms." She had long blond hair and naturally rosy cheeks, bright blue eyes and a voice like Marilyn Monroe's.

"Hi, Jon. Lea's not quite ready yet. Come in."

Jon walked in from the cold and sighed. "Thanks, Ms. Black."

"How's the music going?" she asked, looking at his guitar. "When are you going to come by and play for me?"

"I've written a dozen songs. Lea has a tape. Have you listened to it?"

"Are you saying you won't play a special concert just for me?" she asked and walked close enough to Jon to make him back up against the door. Ms. Black laughed.

Jon blushed and smiled. He hated it when adults talked to him about his music. They always treated him like some dumb kid, and, even worse, Ms. Black made him uncomfortable in ways he'd rather not admit.

"I have to get ready for work. Bye, Jon," she said, before disappearing up the stairs.

Jon took out his guitar and walked into the living room. He felt at home in Lea's house and sat on the couch. He started picking, just to see how in tune the guitar was. Then he adjusted the capo and played "Angel" by Aerosmith. A part of him wished he could play it for Karen, maybe then she'd see him as more than the school nerd.

Lea finally strolled downstairs twenty-five minutes later. She walked into the living room as he played, swaying her hips and bobbing her head to the tune. She wasn't the same girl she was last year. Over the summer she'd grown curvy and had even visited a stylist in the city who straightened her natural curly blond locks. Gone were her tomboy outfits. Now she sported trendy Ts and over-sized sweaters.

"It's about time. What took you so long?" Jon said, returning his guitar to its case.

"I had to . . ."

Together they said, ". . . put on my face."

"Next time put it on earlier," said Jon. "We're going to be late."

"Whatever. We'll take the Jeep."

"Forgiven! It's freezing outside."

CHAPTER THREE

S hortly before 9 a.m. Jon stood by his locker, alone again, figuring out what books he'd need. He was fairly sure it was Day Two, so that meant he had History followed by Sociology. Unless it was Day Three, in which case he had Sociology first. Jon turned to see if there was anyone around he could ask. In mid-spin, he felt a hand on his chest push him against the lockers.

"Did you bring my lunch money?" Nick asked.

"Yeah," Jon whispered.

"What? Couldn't hear you. C'mon, speak like a man."

"Yeah," Jon said a little louder.

"Good boy. I've trained you well." Nick let him go and patted his head as if he were a dog. "Y'know, if you'd just kept your eyes on your dorky friends instead of my cheerleaders, we'd have left you alone this year."

Right. Jon took the money from his pocket and handed it over. Nick smiled, laughed, and, before leaving, patted Jon's head again.

"What a jerk." Jon turned back to his locker.

"Perhaps you should stand up to him."

The dark, raspy voice startled Jon. A few lockers down a new kid, short and muscular, stuffed a huge duffel bag into a locker. His hair was black and hung past his shoulders. His breaths sounded like quiet growls.

"Whatever," Jon muttered. "Are you new?"

The stranger took off his leather jacket. Underneath he was wearing a white muscle shirt that he more than filled out. He looked at Jon, tilting his head the same way that Cosmo did when sizing up someone new. He turned back to his locker. "I must be," he answered.

Jon held out his hand. When the new kid didn't take it, Jon lowered his hand. "I'm Jon Pyre."

The new kid closed his locker and secured it with a padlock. He turned to face Jon and stared at him beneath his low brow. Jon started to back away. He was relieved when the new kid turned and walked down the hall.

"Okay," Jon whispered to himself. "Someone else to make my life miserable. And I still don't know what Day it is."

He sighed and felt a hand on his shoulder. Startled, he turned to face Lea.

"Relax!" she said. "What's got you so jumpy?"

"Nothing." He wished he could tell her about Nick, but being bullied was tough enough on his ego. "Did you see the new kid?"

"What new kid?"

"The guy that just walked out of the alcove? You must've seen him."

Lea shrugged. "Maybe you're still jumpy because of what happened to Mike last week."

"I still say it's weird that a wolf attacked him. Wolves don't usually come near the town, let alone attack people." Jon didn't really want to continue the conversation. Death was not a fun subject. He waited for her to say something, and when she didn't he asked, "What Day is it?"

"Day Five. You have a spare."

"Really? I thought it was either Day Two or Three. I could've slept in."

"Honestly, Pyre. Sometimes you are so absent-minded." She laughed. "I was going to tell you this morning, but you were kind of rude."

"I'll get even."

"Hey, uh, listen. I have something to ask you."

This was it. Lea was going to ask him to the dance. She smiled and stared at her feet. Jon blushed and felt his heart quicken. Should he say yes?

"I'm thinking of joining cheerleading. Tryouts are after school. Do you want to come watch?"

Cheerleading? The Barbie-squad? With Nick there, the guy who banned him from even looking in the direction of a cheerleader?

"Naw, can't."

"Why?" she whined.

"I . . . I've got to work." Not until tomorrow, but he hoped she wouldn't remember.

"I thought you didn't work until tomorrow."

"I don't." *Darn! Think fast, Jon.* "My parents want me to do chores at home. Besides, if I stayed late after school . . ."

Together they said, ". . . my parents would kill me."

Then Jon said solo, "I could phone and ask permission."

"Whatever. Anytime you ask permission for anything it's a guaranteed 'no.'"

Actually, Jon counted on that in times such as this. "Well,

there's the warning buzzer. You'd better get to class."

"All right then," Lea said. She bit her lower lip before quickly asking, "Are you going to the dance on Saturday night?"

"I don't know. Why?" Jon blushed again.

"Just wondering," she said before dashing to class.

The halls emptied quickly as the classes filled. Jon grabbed his guitar case and snuck to the janitor's room, which was never locked, and entered. At the far side of the room, behind a row of mops and brooms, was a staircase to the roof. Whenever Jon needed to get away he headed there to find comfort with his music. As long as he didn't play too loudly no one ever heard him, or, if they did, they didn't realize the music was coming from the roof.

Jon headed up the stairs and sat on a chair he'd snuck up there. Resting his Yamaha on his leg, he began strumming and let the chords carry him off to a place where Nick Bender was a wimp, he was a jock, and Karen Burrard was his girlfriend. He played, and dreamed and escaped, until a voice interrupted him. "Jon!"

Jon stood and spun around. The new kid, the one he'd just met by his locker, was standing behind him with crossed arms.

The stranger leaned against the only exit and said, "Please excuse my imprudence. I didn't mean to frighten you."

Jon reminded himself this wasn't a teacher. "No worries. How did you get up here?"

"I saw you enter the closet and followed. This is a good place for solitude." The stranger walked around, gazing over the endless prairies.

Not anymore, Jon thought. "Yeah. Listen, I don't mean to be rude, but I just wanted to come up here on my spare and practice."

"I need your help."

"With?" Jon clutched his guitar as the stranger stepped up so close that they stood face to face.

"I need you to show me around."

"This is pretty much it," Jon said. What he wanted to say was, "You're rude and freak me out a little," but that would probably get him beaten up.

"Please," the new kid said and crossed his arms. Jon realized by the glare he received that saying no was not an option.

"Fine. You gonna at least tell me your name?" Jon asked as he grabbed his guitar case and started packing up.

"River. River Kitch," he said and slowly extended his hand. Jon paused before taking it. He winced at the strong grip.

They walked down the stairs and, before leaving the closet, Jon peeked into the hallway to make sure there were no teachers. When the coast was clear, he led River into the hall and showed him the library. No one but Mr. Pausron, the new librarian, and a couple Whittaker orphans were inside. Jon turned towards the gym but was stopped by River's voice.

"Who are they?"

"Beverley and Robert. They're orphans, brought here by Whittaker. Kind of an experimental project to help troubled kids."

River glared at them. "Beverley . . . Robert . . ."

"Do you want to meet them?" Jon asked.

"No," River said and pushed past him towards the gym. Jon ran to catch up and lead again. They went to the gym where a class was playing basketball, and from the door they stared in through a glass window.

"This is the gym, a.k.a. Pain Central, as I like to call it."

"Who is that? The Whittaker orphan in there?"

Jon stared at the new kid. Then he looked in through the glass and saw Paul shoot a basket, scoring his team two points. *How do you know he's a Whittaker orphan?*

"That's Paul. He just moved here in the middle of the summer."

"And there are no other orphans in there?" River asked without looking away from the glass.

Jon looked around the hall for any teachers, this time hoping he might see one. "No," he answered. Almost immediately River stepped away from the door and continued down the hall. *Do you want a tour of the school, or the orphans?* Jon wondered as they headed to the cafeteria.

"That's about it," Jon said. "This is the caf, where we go eat. Obviously."

River walked inside and sat at a table in a corner. At the other end of the cafeteria, Nick and his crew occupied three tables, laughing loudly and horsing around. Behind them an orange and black poster was pinned to the wall. Crawling out of a pumpkin was a skeleton with the caption: Are you going to the Halloween Dreams Dance?

"Who are they?" River asked.

Jon walked to the table and rested his guitar against a chair before sitting. "They're just the jocks. Are you

Whittaker's newest orphan?"

River smiled and said, "No."

"Oh. So why did your parents move to the edge of the universe?"

"None of them are orphans? What about that one?" River pointed to Karen. He pointed directly at Karen!

"Dude!" Jon grabbed the new kid's hand and lowered it. "You don't just point at Karen Burrard when Nick could be watching!"

"Is she an orphan?"

"Yeah." Jon looked over his shoulder to see if any of the team had noticed the new kid pointing at them. A few of them were standing at the counter and ordering snacks. Jon watched them awhile, and once he felt at ease, he said, "Quite honestly, if you want to fit in, you probably shouldn't be sitting with me."

"I have no intention of fitting in," River said and stood. He stared once more at Karen, then headed out the door.

After school ended, Lea stood in a cluster of girls who were dressed in purple miniskirts, gold stockings and yellow T-shirts with large purple Fs sewn on the front. She examined the crowd that had gathered on the old, rickety wooden bleachers: the basketball team, a few gawkers from the chess club, but no Pyre. Lea sighed and turned back to the other girls.

"Okay, ladies! Get ready to strut your stuff!" Karen Burrard, the head cheerleader, yelled.

Lea jumped in line, finding herself in the middle. That seemed about right as she didn't want to be first and find out everyone else's routines totally differed from hers, but neither did she want to be last and be compared to everyone else. If she could get into this crowd and get invited to all the great parties, maybe Jon would see her as more than just a "buddy." He might see her the way he saw Karen.

The first girl did a back-flip, cartwheel and the Chinese splits. The second did much the same, except for an added cartwheel. Lea watched the third, the fourth, and then her turn came. She breathed deeply for courage.

Taking a few steps, she bent over and braced her palms on the floor. Kicking her feet high into the air, she flipped over backwards and landed in the Chinese splits.

"Oh yeah!" rose a cheer from the crowd.

Lea looked up hoping to see Pyre, but instead she saw the point guard, Nick. She'd heard some bad things about him, the worst being that he only wanted one thing from girls. She wondered what it was about him that attracted girls yet couldn't help blushing as he continued to cheer. Why couldn't she stop smiling?

"He likes you," Karen said, as Lea walked by her.

Lea smiled. "He's not my type."

Sandra, who had been Lea's best friend in fifth grade, laughed and said to the other girls, "She thinks Karen's serious!"

Sandra turned to Lea. "Honey, he only goes after cheerleaders, and a cheerleader you're not!"

Sandra had said it loudly enough so that everyone heard, even the chess club boys. Lea wanted to cry, but was not about to give her the satisfaction. Holding back her tears, she marched stoically across the gym toward the exit. Why hadn't Pyre come to support her?

"Hey, babe! Where ya goin'?" a voice called out from behind.

The exit was only a few feet away. Reluctantly she turned, hoping whoever it was wouldn't notice that she was about to cry. It was Nick, standing tall and straight with his hands tucked tight into his letterman's jacket and his mullet loose over his shoulders. She looked into his blue eyes and smiled.

"I'm going home. This whole cheerleading thing was pretty lame. I'm not a cheerleader." She tried to chuckle, but her voice wavered.

"Lame?" Nick walked to her, reached out and tenderly stroked her cheek. She blushed. "You're the best they got. If you don't cheer, they better start looking for a new point guard."

"Whatever." Lea couldn't help but smile.

"There's only one way to stop me from quitting." Nick stepped back and winked.

"And what would that be?"

He cocked his head and narrowed his eyes, his innocent smile masking the danger that lurked from within them. "Be a cheerleader and cheer for me."

Lea tried to avoid his gaze but couldn't. "I'm no cheerleader."

"That's a shame."

Lea kept smiling. "Why?"

"Because I was hoping that a certain cute cheerleader would ask me to the dance."

"What makes you think I'd ask you?" she asked coyly,

a little surprised at how natural flirting came to her. But, considering who her mother was, it was probably genetic.

Nick smiled at her before turning back to the cheerleaders. "Hey, Karen! We need to talk!"

November 8, 1998.

I remember the first vampyre I ever staked. She was cocky. I think she was even playing a game with me. As for me, well, I was scared. Plain and simple, I reeked of fear. But I staked her.

It isn't like the movies where they suddenly blow up into dust. Of all the vamps I've killed, I'd say very few of them have ever "dusted." Mostly they die the same as you and me. That is, in a very grotesque, non-Hollywood kind of way.

Don't misunderstand me. Not everything you see in Hollywood movies is made up. I have seen them turn to fog, but it's a fighting technique they use. Rarely do they continue hand-to-hand once they realize I'm no ordinary human. What other powers they have is a mystery to me. I don't know if they can hypnotize or change into wolves or bats. I have no idea where fact meets fiction.

I wish I could say my ignorance comes from a lack of training. It doesn't. I had a vampyre master, a Sage, tutor me even before I became this Defender. His stories came to me in the form of apparitions, unfolding while I was still awake. I mistook the dreams as lies; I didn't think they deserved my attention.

Now I would do anything to dream again.

CHAPTER FOUR

Long grass, chipped white paint, boarded-up windows. *No one would have even noticed the graffiti,* Jon thought as he stared at the center. Cosmo sat at his side with a stick in his mouth. Jon leaned down and scratched his dog's ears. "Stay here and wait. If he turns into some sort of perv, you come in and rescue me." Cosmo nudged the stick into Jon's chest and gave a little bark.

Walking to the door, Jon stared at the brass knocker, debating if he should just go home and confess to his parents what he'd done. *It's not like they'd call the cops, would they?* Could he go to jail for this? No. No way. He hadn't actually done anything, right? He tried the handle and found the door unlocked. *I guess it's better than being traded for cigarettes in Juvi,* Jon concluded as he walked inside.

The clubhouse was as grungy on the inside as it was on the outside. Four teens sat on plastic fold-out chairs in a semicircle with Whittaker at the head. Jon recognized them from school – Paul, Robert, Beverley . . . and Karen, sitting between Robert and Beverley, wearing her trademark miniskirt, tank-top and over-sized sweater that hung off one shoulder. *Of course! Karen's an orphan!* Jon thought gleefully, suddenly not so upset at having to be there.

"Welcome, Jon," Whittaker said. "Take a seat."

"Okay," Jon answered, not seeing any empty chairs.

Karen sighed and said, "You know, the sooner you sit, the sooner we can all get out of here."

Don't panic, Jon thought. Paul stood and handed him his chair before sitting on the floor himself. Jon took the chair and smiled a thank-you. Then he quickly looked at Karen, who rolled her eyes.

"Good show of selflessness, Paul!" Whittaker praised him. "You're doing very well for your second month in the program."

"Thanks, Mr. Whittaker. Some days it's harder to leave behind my old ways."

"Now, onto business," Mr. Whittaker said. "Conway groceries has an opening for an after school clerk. Who would like to apply?"

"Mike's body isn't even cold! The killer, the wolf, is still out there!" Karen spat.

"Mr. Conway still needs our help. Would Mike have wanted us to forget that?"

Jon knew no one else in the town would work with "loser" Conway. And who could blame them? He was a drunk. The only reason people shopped at Conway Groceries was because it was a two-hour drive to the next grocer.

"I'll do it," Beverley volunteered.

"Thank-you, Beverley. Just do be careful, and don't walk home alone. Now I need two volunteers to clean up Sunset Park." Whittaker stared directly at Karen as he said, "It seems there's been some parties there, and those responsible have littered the park with beer bottles."

"I'll do it," Paul volunteered.

"I can help," Robert said. Whittaker smiled at Karen, who seemed reluctant to help with anything. "That leaves you and Jon to help with cleaning up the After Dusk. Tonight, you can tend the lawn."

They all stared at Jon, and Whittaker laughed. "I know it seems strange that Jon is not an orphan like you. But, like you, he wants to make sure that he stays on the right path. Welcome him my children, for tonight he shall become like a brother among you."

Chills stabbed at Jon's spine when Whittaker said, "like a brother among you."

"Yeah, I'm just here tonight, Friday and Saturday. After Saturday, I'm done here," Jon rambled, as everyone got up and headed for the kitchen.

Paul patted him on the shoulder and said, "C'mon. First we eat, then we work."

The kitchen was just off the main room and was barely big enough for a stove, fridge, sink and table for eight. When they all sat, Jon found himself across from Karen, who kept curling her upper lip at him and fixing her sweater to cover more of her bare shoulder. *Nick is going to kick my butt,* Jon thought. It was hot, that elderly-crank-the-heat-full-blast kind of hot. That's when Jon noticed a fire burning in a wood stove.

As Whittaker placed bowls of stew in front of each teen, they all started eating. Jon picked at his with a spoon. It looked like the stuff he fed Cosmo, with pasty gravy and chunks of gray meat. There was a red film on top that looked like tomato soup.

"Yeah, you know what? I'm not hungry." Jon pushed the bowl away.

"That would leave you more time for chores, certainly," Whittaker said. "While we are eating, how would you like to scrub the bathroom?"

Jon hated the innocent, matter-of-fact way that Whittaker spoke to him. What he hated even more was that everyone else snickered. His shoulders slumped and he gave in. "Fine. I'll eat."

Steam from the meat rose above the bowl and into Jon's nose. It smelled like his mother's stew. He took another whiff, and a shock wave hit his temples. He felt a little lightheaded and coughed. He took a taste of the gravy from the spoon. *Bland as Mom's.* Instantly, his entire body warmed and his pulse quickened. The sensation lasted for less than a second. *Mom's doesn't do that!*

Shoving a full scoop into his mouth, Jon chewed fast and swallowed. It invigorated him. He felt powerful, as if nothing could stand in his way. Again, this emotion lasted for only the time it took him to swallow the stew. As he ate more, the sensations grew stronger and lasted longer.

When everyone was finished their dinner, Beverley started taking the plates away. Robert gathered plastic bags to clean up Sunset Park, while Karen sneered at Jon.

"Well, *brother Jon,* I hope you enjoyed your stew," Karen said. "Shall we do our chores now?"

Whittaker got up and grabbed his coat. Before leaving he said, "Remember kids. You don't do what you do to serve your ends. You do what you do because it is right. In the end, what is right will serve you."

Then he left. Beverley grabbed her coat and headed for the door, "See you later, suckers! My servitude won't start for at least a week! Tonight, I have a date with the love of my life!"

Jon watched her leave. Karen threw Jon his jacket and said, "Push mower's under the house."

"He doesn't have a gas one?" Jon asked.

Karen rolled her eyes.

"Great," Jon said as he followed her out of the bungalow. "Just great."

CHAPTER FIVE

The sun had begun to set as Jon waded through the grass until he stared into the dark crawl space beneath the house. He couldn't see a push mower. Cosmo tried to force his way beside Jon, as if this were a hide and seek game. To get him out of the way, Jon found a stick and threw it across the lawn. Cosmo ran after it, barking.

"This isn't a game, Pyre," Karen said. "Stop goofing around and get the mower."

Jon hated Whittaker for doing this to him. *My only chance to show Karen who I really am, and I'm stuck doing chores for an old man?* He turned back to the crawlspace, reached in through the cobwebs and felt around in the shadows. When he touched something that felt like a push mower's handle, he yanked as hard as he could until he dragged it out. The mower came more easily than he thought, and he stumbled backwards, falling on his butt.

Karen laughed.

Jon stood up and brushed himself off. His faced burned with embarrassment. "I play the guitar, y'know," he blurted out. *Nice segue,* Jon thought.

"Is that supposed to impress me? Should I swoon and be your girlfriend?"

"Uh, no. I just thought . . ."

"Cut the grass!"

Jon started pushing the ancient mower over the unkempt lawn. Cosmo ran around him, barking as the mower spewed out clipped grass. Karen leaned against the house and watched. "I hate dogs," she said.

Jon snapped, "Are you going to weed the garden or not?"

"Not. What kind of name is 'Pyre,' anyway?"

"It's my last name. If you do the garden while I do this we'll get done faster."

"I'm more of a voyeur than a doer. At least with chores . . ."

At least we're talking, he thought.

"It means to burn bodies as a funeral rite." Karen stared at her nails. "She calls you 'Pyre,' doesn't she?"

Jon stopped mowing. "What? Who?"

"Lea. She tried out for cheerleading."

"I guess. She's a cheerleader now?"

"Only because it was easier saying yes to Nick than saying no to her."

Jon felt his face burn when she mentioned that name. *Why am I such a loser?*

Karen laughed. "Keep mowing. Why are you so afraid of Nick?"

"I didn't say I was afraid."

Karen walked up to Jon and placed her hand flush against his chest. His heart raced as she said, "I'm far more attracted to a man with bruises than a boy with fair skin."

She's touching me! Karen is touching me!

"Later, Jon."

"Uh, we're not done yet."

As she started across the street, she yelled back, "No, *you're* not done yet."

Jon started mowing again. "At least she talked to me," he mumbled.

By the time Jon finished the lawn it was well past dark. He looked at the garden, with all the weeds still intact, and whispered, "I'll do them Friday." He pulled the mower back to the crawlspace but stopped when Cosmo ran in front of him. Before Jon could grab a stick to throw, a burning sensation erupted in his stomach. Falling to his knees, he held his arms tightly to his chest and curled into a ball. Cosmo sat beside him and licked his face.

Suddenly the air turned cold and the ground quaked. Jon braced himself by holding onto Cosmo until he couldn't feel his dog's licks. Mountains began to rise far in the horizon, casting a dark shadow into what became a valley around him. His dog disappeared, and the houses morphed into trees.

Another mountain rose up from the earth, causing Jon to stagger as he stood. He watched, strangely calm, as a cavern appeared like a wide yawn right before him. Rock formations hung from the ceiling like fangs, and a cobblestone walkway jutted forth like a serpent's tongue. The mountain rose high against the overcast sky, and two crags jetted off like bat wings. There was a sound of water nearby, heavy waves lashing against rocks.

Three teen boys appeared around him, each of them immersed in a gray fog that drifted into the valley. He somehow knew what they were called: the Broadsword

Fellows. As his vision adapted to the fog, Jon recognized the three boys as the Whittaker orphans, Robert, Mike and Paul. *Mike! You're alive!* Jon wanted to cry out to him.

"Just how brave is the mighty Liam Whittaker?" the boy who looked exactly like Robert asked. Jon looked down at himself and saw that he was wearing a heavy mail suit and a flowing red cape.

He tried to speak, but when he opened his mouth laughter came out. It was not his voice, yet it was his eyes that stared into the cave.

"And what will I find here?" Liam asked, anxiously. Jon was present only as a spirit, as if experiencing first-hand someone else's dream.

The boy who looked strikingly like Mike handed him a heavy leather satchel. "Vampyres. In there, you will find the unholy."

Liam's shoulders relaxed. He sighed and almost laughed. "Vampyres? Why not give me a test of courage that is real?"

Mike grabbed the satchel back. "Perhaps you won't need this?" Mike taunted.

"How brave is the Mighty Liam?" Paul's twin asked, repeating Robert's words.

"I am the bravest among us, and I am not afraid of the lore of superstitious villagers!" Liam shouted, snatching his satchel back and giving Robert a shove. "I shall go into that cave, and if I find anyone at home may Those Who Protect Us help them!"

"But you do not believe in Those Who Protect Us. What will you do, should you encounter a creature of the night?"

Liam walked a few paces toward the mouth and stopped.

He turned to the others, cocked a smile and said, "I'll drive a stake into his navel and bring his heart back in this satchel."

Throwing his shoulders back, he held his head high and strode up the cobblestone walkway. A breeze groaned from within the cavern. Liam stiffened as he stepped one foot inside, as if he were stepping into a cold lake. Closing his eyes and holding his breath he jumped, immersing himself inside the strange air.

As he journeyed down the narrow corridor, Liam searched the satchel for a torch but found none. He looked about and noticed that, unlike the entrance, these walls were flawless and adorned with oil lamps in golden sconces. He walked close to one, but when the lamp suddenly ignited he jumped back. His heart pounded. Slowly he drew closer to the flaming lamp.

The sconce was a human skeletal hand nailed to the wall at the wrist, with the rest of the skeleton partially melted into the stone wall. Where eyes had once been there were now deep, empty sockets and the jaw was stretched open, as if the person had died screaming in pain.

"That was a tasty one," a voice bellowed from farther in the cavern.

Liam swiveled around. "I am Liam the Mighty!" he shouted.

Low laughter bounced from wall to wall mixing with the breeze that whistled through the tunnel. Liam reached into his satchel and pulled out a wooden stake. He slung the leather bag back over his shoulder with one hand, the stake shaking in his other.

Liam stepped back once, then twice . . . then he stopped.

"There are no vampyres," he said loudly. "This is a ruse intended to discredit me."

He leaped forward, farther into the cavern. Every lamp he passed ignited, each displaying a skeletal corpse encased from within the stone wall.

At the end of the passageway, the cave opened into a Great Hall complete with marble floors and whitewashed walls. A diamond-crested chandelier, decorated with candles that shone as brightly as the sun outside, hung from the roof. Seven winding staircases, three to the east, three to the west, and one to the north, led to a balcony surrounding the room. Atop each stairwell stood a dark, cloaked figure.

"I am Liam the Mighty!" he shouted, as if to remind himself more than to unnerve those at whom he yelled.

A dozen giant bats swooped at him from the ceiling, knocking the stake from his hand. Liam raised his arms to ward off the winged demons, and once they passed he turned to the entryway where a dozen cloaked men blocked his escape.

Suddenly Jon was pulled out from Liam and cast into darkness. He heard a faint bark and concentrated on it, letting Cosmo bring him back to reality. He forced his eyes open and saw that snow had begun to fall, dusting his clothing and hair. There was no cave, no mountains and no sound of lashing waves. There was only a freshly cut lawn, a dilapidated community center and a dog with worried eyes.

"Thanks, buddy. I'm okay. I think," Jon whispered as he forced himself to stand up, brushing the snow from his clothing. His legs were shaky. He pressed his fingers against his temples and wondered what had happened. *Did I hit my head?* He looked at his dog. "Maybe you and I should take a walk."

Cosmo ran for a stick and brought it back to his master. Jon took it and threw it. As they walked, houses changed into offices and stores. Main Street was lined with all the essentials: Leo's General Store, Hank's Post Office, Jenny's Stationary and Gift Store, the police station and fire hall. *Everything you could ever need,* as his mom always said. *So long as you don't need it past 6 p.m.,* Jon thought. The town completely closed down at six, except for Icy Shakes and their local theater, Famous Productions. Jon noticed that *The Lost Boys* was playing. *Huh. Minitaw is now only two years behind the rest of the world.* He also noticed Nick's van parked outside the theater and figured it was best to stay out of sight.

Just as he was about to turn down a side street, a 1979 Datsun station wagon, bright orange in color, drove down the strip. Jon watched it roll past, wondering where his dad was going at such a late hour. He jogged in the direction of the car, and Cosmo trotted behind, happy for what he seemed to think was a game. Jon's dad drove all the way out to Sunset Park. Another vehicle pulled in shortly after. It was Lea's Jeep!

Jon crouched behind a bush and reached for Cosmo's collar. Jon was too far away to hear what was going on, but he didn't dare creep closer and risk getting caught. His dad and Ms. Black got out of their vehicles. His dad brought Ms. Black close and kissed her long and hard.

"C'mon, Cosmo. It's time to go home," he choked.

CHAPTER SIX
OCTOBER 26TH, 1989. THURSDAY.

J on woke from the impact of Cosmo's paws landing in his stomach. He sat upright, receiving a sloppy kiss followed by a loud bark. Clamping Cosmo's mouth shut, he looked at his clock that had been buzzing for the last ten minutes.

"Shh, you're going to get us in trouble . . . but thanks for waking me up," Jon said. He still felt half-asleep. His head was pounding and his throat was dry. He desperately needed a drink.

Cosmo barked again. "Okay, okay," Jon said, as he crawled out of bed and pulled on his jeans and T-shirt. When he opened his bedroom door, he saw his dad just about to go into the bathroom. His father stopped and glared at him.

"Uh, what's up?" Jon asked quietly.

"I worked late last night and would have appreciated sleeping in this morning," his dad replied through tight lips.

"Sorry." Jon tried to walk past.

Why you're tired has nothing to do with working late.

His dad pushed Jon back into his room, and Cosmo let out a low growl.

"I'd suggest you get that mutt under control before I lose my temper."

This was the part in the conversation where Jon usually pleaded to his father for leniency. However, as the hair on his arms stood on end, he felt a surge of energy flow through his veins. Cosmo started whining and spinning in a circle.

"And what are you going to do about it?" Jon asked.

"Decided to try having a spine? Or are you hoping to wake your mother so she'll come protect you?"

"What kind of insurance papers did you need to give Ms. Black last night at Sunset Park?"

"What?" His dad took a step backwards, confirming what Jon suspected.

"Last night. Sunset Park. 10 p.m." Jon paused. "Do you want to get out of my room now?"

Jon couldn't believe what he'd just said, or that his father actually backed away and let him pass. Cosmo nudged him down the stairs.

Jon zipped up his parka. Cosmo ran from tree to tree, making sure each one belonged to him. A block down, the Parkers had decorated their lawn to look like a cemetery with gravestones and a skeleton crawling out of the dirt. Cosmo ran over to sniff it.

"Hey, Jon!" Paul shouted from his second floor bedroom window.

Jon waved and started to walk again. Paul had moved into the Parker's house only six weeks ago, but had never spoken to him. In fact, usually Paul seemed to go out of his way to avoid him.

"Jon!" Paul shouted again. "Wait up!"

"Okay," Jon said, as Cosmo marked a cemetery plot.

Paul was down in a few minutes. "Mind if I walk with you?"

"It's a free country."

They continued down the block without talking. Finally Paul asked, "So what's Whittaker got on you?"

"What do you mean?"

Paul laughed. "I'm sure you're the nicest guy in the world, Jon. But do you expect me to believe you're fixing up our youth center out of goodwill?

Jon lost his breath and heard something click in the back of his mind. He couldn't stop himself from snarling as he said, "Why don't you mind your own business!"

Paul threw up his hands and took a few steps back. "Whoa! We all come to Whittaker for redemption, buddy. No shame in it."

Whatever switch had gone off in Jon's mind flipped back to its normal position. "Sorry. I . . . I don't know what came over me."

"No worries," Paul said, patting Jon on the back. Before turning to go home, he added, "I just wanted to welcome you to the After Dusk. You're the only one I feel cool with. I hope you'll stay. We need you, Jon."

"Yeah, later," Jon said as they went their separate ways, thinking to himself, *Weird*.

Dodgeball was the bane of Jon's life. And they played this psycho's-excuse-for-a-sport every sixth school day, and usually it was the older boys against the younger boys. The first time Jon had played the game he had thought it might be fun, until the first volleyball smacked him on the side of the head.

He'd walked around with a red welt over his left eye for a week.

But Jon had learned an easy way out. He'd stand near the front, usually close to where Nick was, wait for someone to get a ball and stay still. The sooner he got hit, the sooner he could go sit on the bleachers and daydream about Karen. It wasn't like he cared what these guys thought of him.

"Men! We're going to make this game interesting today." Like most phys-ed teachers, Coach Tannis sounded like a rejected marine. "The girls are joining us for this class."

Jon stiffened as the girls poured into the gym. They had but one duty: to form a human barrier around the boys and snatch a ball to give to a boy of their choice. Jon had heard of the coach doing this once, but up until now he had thought it was just an urban legend.

"My life is hell," Jon muttered, glancing behind him to see Lea waving.

Jon heard two of the boys next to him whispering, "Lea really filled out this year." He noticed she wasn't wearing baggy sweats and a sweatshirt, her usual gym clothes. She was wearing short shorts and a very tight T-shirt. *Wow. She actually looks cute.* Jon immediately wiped that thought from his mind as Karen walked in.

She was dressed in the same short shorts as Lea, but because she was taller she had more leg to show. Her complexion was lighter than the other girls and made even more so against her dark hair. While that might not have worked for most girls, Karen had a way of moving through the crowd that made every boy weak in the knees. Especially Jon.

The game! I need to concentrate on the game! Jon thought as Coach Tannis yelled, "Man your territory!"

Jon moved closer to the middle of the group. He remembered what Karen had said last night, *"I'm far more attracted to a man with bruises than a boy with fair skin,"* and vowed he wouldn't be the first hit. This was his chance to show Karen that he was her kind of guy! He was shorter than everyone else, so how tough could it be to hide behind them? Ten guys on his side, eleven on the other. He could at least last a short while, or so he thought, until he saw that Nick's eyes were fixed on him.

"You can do it, Pyre," Lea called to him.

"Great," he whispered, "she's drawing more attention to me."

Coach Tannis threw in eight volleyballs, and immediately they began flying about the gym like the balls in a mad pinball machine. The first of many balls hurtled towards him. Diving to the floor, Jon dodged it. *I actually dodged it!*

He jumped to his feet. There was something odd about the way the balls flew towards him. It was as if they were under water, as if they were slowed down by a thickening of the air. He saw one come toward him and easily ducked beneath it. At almost the same second, another hurtled toward him, and he bent over backwards, avoiding it, too. It was now nine-eleven, and Jon was still in the game.

Each time a ball came his way it slowed, and he stepped aside. He even grabbed a couple balls, not caught so much as simply plucked them from the air, and hurtled them at his opponents. He tagged two. With every dodge and every tag, Jon's bravado increased. *I'm actually going to win this thing!* But when he found himself alone on his side, with two boys on the other, one of which was Nick, his fear returned.

Uh, oh. What if Nick takes this out on me later? Jon considered giving up. He thought about letting Nick or the other guy, Bob, tag him. But when he heard Lea call him instinct took over. He turned to see the ball she had thrown to him, and catching it he hurtled it. The ball hit Bob in the chest so hard he stumbled. "Tag!" Bob wheezed. Nick grabbed a ball and dribbled it, his scowl fixed on Jon.

So it was just the two of them.

Again Jon heard Lea shout as she threw him a ball. Energy surged into Jon, and when he pitched the ball it flew so fast that it made a loud whoosh! Nick didn't have time to react. The ball hit him in the chest and he staggered backwards from the impact.

"Holy crap, I won!" Jon said with amazement. "I won!"

Nick grabbed the ball and rubbed his chest. Although he'd lost, he still threw it back at Jon. Smashing him in the nose. Sending him flat on his butt.

The gym echoed with laughter as Jon shook his aching head in a vain attempt to regain his senses. Licking his lips, he tasted blood, and pinching his nostrils, he stopped his nosebleed.

"Are you okay?" Lea asked.

"Yeah."

Lea looked at Nick. "What's your problem?"

"I just reacted, sorry man." Nick gave Jon a glare that indicated he'd better accept the apology.

"No worries. I'm not hurt."

"It doesn't look like it to me!" Coach Tannis barked, throwing him an ice pack and towel. "Get off the floor and clean yourself up."

Lea grabbed Jon's arm and helped him off the floor. As they wandered over to the bleachers, the coach set things up for a co-ed volleyball game. Lea held the ice-pack to Jon's nose. Strangely, he didn't feel any pain.

"I think I'm good," Jon said.

"I don't mind staying with you. You were awesome!"

"It's just Dodgeball." *Did my voice just squeak?* "Lea, you're kind of embarrassing me." He pushed away the ice-pack.

"I'm just being your friend."

"Whatever," Jon said. He tried to look anywhere but at her. She definitely looked different this year, and it was obvious by the way all the guys were staring that he wasn't the only one who noticed.

"Hey, ask me about cheerleading," Lea said with an edge to her voice.

"Are you really on the Barbie-squad?"

"Oh. So Karen's a cheerleader, but I'm a Barbie?"

"I didn't mean it like that." He still couldn't look at her. She slowly let go of the ice-pack from his face, and he reached up to catch it before it fell. Their hands touched briefly, and suddenly Jon felt that cold flash again.

"Nick stuck up for me and got me on the squad."

"Nick?"

"Yeah." She smiled and looked over to Nick. Jon could feel his cheeks burning, and for the first time was speechless with her. "Since you're so good here, maybe I'll just go over to him," she added.

"Maybe you should, then," he said, as she stood to leave. She waited a few seconds as if giving Jon time to stop her. When he didn't, she stormed off.

Nick watched Jon and Lea while he and his gang set up a volleyball net.

"I can't believe that nerd nailed me," Bob said. "I can't believe that nerd nailed you!"

"I can't believe that babe is with him," Nick said, as he finished securing one side of the net.

"Lea?" Sandra said.

"She's a waste of time," Karen added.

Nick jumped from the chair and walked over to her. Brushing back her long, dark hair, he asked, "When are you going to learn I really am God's gift to women?"

"You're such a jerk," Karen said, pushing him away.

"Does anyone else think I can't get her?" Nick challenged the group.

"I do hear the glove drawn," Bob asked.

"That's 'gauntlet thrown,' you idiot," Karen said.

"Two dates. I'll have her by the second date," Nick said.

"Here she comes," Sandra said, as she spied Lea behind them.

Nick tossed Lea a volleyball. "Babe! You're on my team!"

November 10, 1998.

When I first started to change it never occurred to me that vampyres might be behind it. I think I would have been more willing to accept that my parents had found me in a spaceship that crashed during a green meteor shower.

But there were changes happening to me because of an experiment conducted by vampyres. On the one hand, it frightened the hell out of me. On the other, it gave me the upper hand where before I had none.

It surprises even me what I accepted to get that upper hand. It shocks me to think of the person I became once I got it.

CHAPTER SEVEN

J on's mind raced to explain how he could have become so agile during Dodgeball. *Maybe it's just puberty*, he thought.

He snuck out of school, heading to a place he liked to go not far from the gas station, under the bridge just outside Sunset Park. It was out of the sun, away from the people in the town. He brought his guitar, his only real escape.

Beneath the bridge it smelled of fish and algae. The Cananee had receded a fair amount since last spring, but it was still a swift-moving river. Jon sat and started to play. As his fingers brushed out the chords, his song carried away his thoughts and worries. Nick Bender . . . Saint Whittaker . . . even the incident with Lea all faded into the music. He cast himself into a world where he was the tough guy, Nick Bender the nerd, and Karen Burrard his girlfriend. It was a world that only his music had the ability to create. Beneath the bridge it felt like no one could touch him.

Then a bang hit his temples. The bridge flew through the air, disappearing into a black sky. The rocky ground beneath him smoothed, and walls appeared around him. His guitar melted into a stake, and a hand that came from nowhere grasped him by the collar.

Jon tried to fight back, but he was no longer in control. Once again he was trapped inside Liam Whittaker's body.

The man that held Liam was wearing a midnight cape that enveloped him like a second skin. Where the garment stopped at the neck, a collar rose like wings. His mouth was partially shielded by the collar but not his bright blue eyes, which looked like crescent moons fallen on their sides. He glared at Liam. "Mighty Liam," he said, his voice deep and loud, "have you ventured so close to death to slay us?"

"I have come to end your darkness!" Liam yelled, pulling a wooden cross from the satchel. *If I'm going to die I may as well go out a hero,* he decided. The vampyre laughed, walking close to the wooden cross.

"This will not protect you. 'Tis not its shape that repels our evil but the faith one has in its meaning. Do you, Mighty Liam, know its meaning?"

"I know better than to believe you!" Liam held the cross closer to the demon. "Back demon! Back!"

The vampyre lifted a finger and the wooden cross burst into flames. Liam yelped, dropped it and turned nearly as pale as the creature he faced. The vampyre laughed.

"Perhaps you should first learn to trust me, or better yet, stop calling me demon. I am Naztar, Sage of this Kith." He paused, kneeling to meet Liam eye to eye. "If I wanted to kill you, I would have done so by now."

"You mean I'm going to live?"

As the demon rose, the air caught his cloak like he might take flight. Walking a few paces, he said, "I never said I'd let you live. I only said you would not die."

The dream of Liam faded away. As Jon came to, he gripped his guitar and felt a trickle of sweat run down his forehead. *Why am I having these visions?*

Suddenly, he heard a voice he recognized: Nick Bender's. "Hey, check it out. A Bridge Nerd."

He hadn't heard Nick's van drive over the bridge, or the Bender crew climb down underneath. But there they were: Bob, Trevor, Nick, Sandra and Karen. *Oh no,* Jon thought, *Karen's going to see Nick beat me up.*

As if sensing that Jon was considering making a run for it, Bob and Trevor blocked the opposite side of the bridge. Nick crossed his arms, glared at Jon and said, "Play me a song. If I like it, I'll let you live."

Jon's hands were still shaking too much to play. He tried and wound up sounding like he'd never picked up a guitar before. Nick sat beside him and leaned in close.

"You play like shit." Nick took away the instrument. "You and I have a problem. You showed me up in gym class."

"I . . . I was just fooling around," Jon muttered.

"I have a rep. Do you know what happens when nerds get the better of me?"

Suddenly Nick stood and swung the guitar towards a support post. But before it hit a hand grabbed it. The hand belonged to River Kitch, the new kid Jon had shown around school. Nick let go of the guitar and stood chest to chest with River. Both boys glared at each other.

"I suggest you turn around and walk away," Nick said.

"I suggest you leave this kid alone," replied River Kitch in a low growl.

That's when Jon's strange powers returned. The Cananee slowed until it almost didn't move. The two boys who were at a standoff looked like stone, and Jon walked over to them. They were moving but so slowly Jon almost couldn't see it. He grabbed his guitar from River's hand and walked back to his spot.

Just as suddenly as it had begun, his super-speed ended. Nick spun around. "How the hell did you get your guitar?"

River Kitch stared at Jon and slowly reached into his jacket. He took out a pair of sunglasses and put them on. A voice that sounded like the stranger's growled in Jon's mind, *Fight back!*

Did he just speak in my mind? Jon wondered as River jumped up onto the bridge and disappeared.

Nick shouted after him, "You better run, coward! When I find you again, I'll teach you the lesson of your life!" He spun back to Jon. "Is that a friend of yours?"

"C'mon Nick," Karen said as Nick grabbed Jon. "This isn't funny anymore."

Nick punched Jon hard in the jaw. Jon fell to the ground and looked up, just in time to see a boot hit his shoulder. Jon landed on his back, onto a rock that jetted out of the ground.

Suddenly, Jon flipped to his feet and punched back. He wasn't sure where the bravery to strike back came from, but when his knuckles hit Nick below the chin, a rush of adrenaline replaced his fear.

Every blade of grass around him smelled pungent; the air seemed fluid. He could even feel the slight change in temperature where the shadow of the bridge blocked out the sun. Jon didn't know and didn't care what was giving him these powers. Nick was actually on his knees, blood dripping from his chin, from a blow that he had delivered!

"You're dead," whispered Nick as he tackled Jon. But this time Jon rolled Nick over and kicked him in the stomach. With a second kick, Nick toppled backwards, right into the river. He hit the water with a splash.

Jon stood and smiled, at least until Trevor and Bob took hold of him. Karen and Sandra yelled at them to stop. Jon grabbed Trevor ... but whatever had given him such power was now gone. Despite his struggles, the boys held him fast. Nick walked out from the water, his clothes soaked tight against his skin. His mullet dripped down his back, and his teeth chattered from the cold. "I'm going to make you wish you were never born," he said and punched Jon right in the nose.

Jon woke to the cool touch of falling snow. He lay on the bank of the Cananee on his back, his head tilted to the side. He tried to open his eyes, and one fluttered open while the other stayed shut. Every breath he took stabbed like a knife.

Jon rolled onto his side and forced himself to stand. He knew he had to get home. He had to get help. Of course, this meant telling his parents about Nick and facing his dad's disappointment that he'd lost a fight. But he had fought back. More than that, he had almost won. *How did I become so strong?*

Dried blood covered cuts and scrapes on his face. He felt his jaw and flinched as his fingers brushed against a lump. Then a rush of water, not from the Cananee but from within his head, filled the silence. It was as if all the blood in his body had suddenly rushed into his temples, making his brain feel like it might burst. It hurt in a way that made Jon think he was going to die. When the pain stopped, he stood up, breathless. He looked at his knuckles and gasped.

The cuts and scrapes were gone. He touched his face. His skin was smooth. The lump on his jaw was gone; the cuts had healed.

"What the hell is happening to me?" he whispered as he grabbed his guitar and ran home.

CHAPTER EIGHT

he Datsun was parked in the driveway, which meant his dad was home. Mom was always home, so hopefully she had taken the school's call when they phoned to ask why he'd missed his afternoon classes. His mom would be disappointed, but she never got as angry as his dad. And it wasn't as if he had an excuse. After all, his story of getting beaten up had lost credibility now that he had healed. Mind you, there were his torn, bloody clothes for proof.

Jon walked in and his mom stormed downstairs.

Here it comes, thought Jon.

"Hi, honey. I thought you were upstairs?" she asked.

"Uh, no . . ." he stammered.

"Are you just getting home from school? Good for you for staying late!"

Jon paused. "Didn't anyone call?"

"Are you expecting a call?"

The school never called? What about work? Jon thought, saying aloud, "My shift started at the gas station a half-hour ago."

"Well, get changed and I'll drive you."

No one missed me, he thought as he ran upstairs. Quickly, he slipped into a fresh T-shirt and jeans. When he came back downstairs, his mom was already in the car with the engine running.

A cold wind rustled through the long prairie grass. The sun had set an hour ago and the sky was alive with stars that looked like tiny specs of ice. Jon hated the cold, and the nights were only getting colder. Farcus Gas consisted of two pumps and a mechanic shop that was open during the weekdays. On weekends the garage was free for the employees to use. Jon sat inside the attendant booth, strumming a soft tune that he'd been writing on and off for two months.

There was a rumble in the distance. He leaned his guitar against the wall, threw on his parka and followed Cosmo outside. Jon watched as a low-riding muscle car approached from the distance, its black paint polished so it reflected the night sky. As it slowed and pulled into the lot, Jon recognized it as a 1972 Barracuda, a car his dad would have gone crazy over. The driver stepped out. It was River Kitch.

"Hey," Jon said, as the new kid took the pump in hand, "it's full-serve."

"I can do it myself," he growled, shoving the nozzle into the car's tank.

"Okay, no worries," Jon said. Then, after a pause, he muttered, "I'm okay, by the way."

River Kitch said nothing. The numbers clicked on the gas pump, the sound echoing in the stillness. Finally, he broke the silence. "What do you know of Whittaker?"

"Huh?" Jon grabbed the squeegee and started wiping

down the windows. *This again?*

"The orphans," River said.

Jon reached down and gave Cosmo a scratch behind the ears to make sure he stayed close.

"Did Conway have contact with these orphans?"

"You mean the guy who owns Conway Groceries?" Jon wasn't sure how much he should say. He thought instantly of Mike's body discovered in the graveyard, and shivered. *Why are you so curious about the orphans?*

The clicking from the pump stopped and the stranger returned the nozzle to its base. Then he walked to Jon and said, "What is Whittaker's connection to him?"

Jon shrugged. "Nothing. Mr. Whittaker just finds him after school help, that's all."

"The orphans?"

"Yeah . . . the kids from the After Dusk."

"Conway was working alone tonight," River said, as if accusing Jon of lying.

"I think Beverley starts next week."

"Beverley . . ." he whispered, handing Jon two twenty dollar bills.

BEEP! blasted a horn from behind as Jon fished for change. Jon jumped, dropped the change and nearly got run over as the Barracuda suddenly took off.

Jon turned to face a sleek black motorbike, a Honda Shadow 1100, with a young woman mounted on its leather seat. She was clad in black leather: tight pants, biker boots, and a heavy jacket adorned with scores of zippers and chains. Her bleached-blond hair hung in a ponytail to the middle of her back. She pulled her gloves tight and crossed her arms. She couldn't have been older than seventeen, barely old enough to drive the bike. Jon wondered where she had come from and where she was going. When she leaned back in her seat, Jon realized he was staring.

"Are you going to jump to the pump, or what?"

"Uh, yeah . . . should I fill 'er up?"

"Only two bucks. And I need a phone."

Jon picked the coins up from off the pavement, then grabbed the pump's handle. He couldn't release himself from her icy stare. She undid her ponytail and brushed her fingers through her long hair.

Slowly and loudly, she repeated, "A . . . phone . . .?"

"Oh, sorry. There's a pay one by the Coke machine." He pointed to it and accidentally hit the pump's button. They both jumped to avoid the gas released by the nozzle.

"I guess I'd better not light up," she muttered as she got off the bike. Jon smiled to hide his nervousness.

"Unbelievable," he whispered when she'd walked away. "It's like hot women are my Kryptonite."

Jon stuck the nozzle into the gas tank and watched the numbers rise. He tried forgetting what a fool he'd been and concentrated on his task. The wind died down and the prairie turned silent, except for the whir of the gas pump . . . and the woman's voice. She was close enough that he could hear her conversation, and although he tried not to listen, he just couldn't help it.

"Yeah, I'm here . . . I got lost, okay? It's not like they've got rest areas every ten miles in this backwards place . . . I haven't seen Whittaker . . . I don't know. Yes, we should worry."

Whittaker, Jon thought. He looked down at Cosmo, who sat by his side. Cosmo gave a loud bark, then ran to a cluster of trees to mark them as his own. *Sounds like Whittaker's in trouble.*

Look at the bike, came a voice in his mind that sounded strangely like River Kitch's.

"Huh?" Jon glanced around to see who had spoken to him.

It's your conscience. Trust me, look at the bike.

He looked down the bike. A rolled-up sleeping bag and tent were tied to the back and on each side were two leather saddlebags.

Open the saddlebags.

"I'm going crazy," Jon muttered, again scanning the empty lot. He flicked open the saddlebag closest to him and immediately wished he hadn't. Handguns, switchblades, brass knuckles and weird metal instruments he couldn't even recognize filled the sack. "Ho-lee shit," he whispered, quickly shutting the satchel.

"HEY KID! I SAID TWO!" She hung up and started towards him, her glare sharp enough to slay any beast.

The pump clicked from sensing the tank was full. The numbers read seven and some change. Though the night was dark enough to hide everything beyond the lights of the gas station, Jon was standing directly beneath the lights. *Did she see me?*

"Sorry. I'll only charge what you asked."

"Darn right you won't charge me full. It's not a good sign for the future when youths today can't even pump gas."

"I said I was sorry."

Her voice turned soft. "Sorry doesn't always cut it, kid. Don't forget that." She gave him two bucks and sounded cold again as she added, "Let's just hope we never meet again."

Jon watched her speed off. As she disappeared into the darkness, the Northern Lights came alive with streaks of pink and green. Jon blinked, wondering if it was all some kind of dream. "Weird," he whispered.

What could she want with Saint Whittaker? Was the old guy in some kind of trouble? More so, what was she doing armed to the teeth in a quiet town like Minitaw? She couldn't be here hunting the renegade wolf, not with switchblades and brass knuckles. Cosmo ran to him and started pushing a stick into his side. Jon grabbed it, gave it a toss, and then walked back to the attendant's booth.

Kevin stared at the untouched burger on his tray. Beverley, sitting across from him, picked at her fries.

"So, it's over, just like that?" Beverley asked, biting her trembling lower lip.

"Yeah," Kevin answered, barely loud enough for her to hear. "Sorry, Bev. I just don't want a girlfriend tying me down during my last year of high school."

Beverley looked around Icy Shakes to see if anyone was listening. There were only a few other kids there, no one who mattered. She looked at Kevin, meeting his dry eyes with her teary gaze. "How can you be so cold about this?"

Kevin opened the tin foil from around his burger and took a bite. Without swallowing he said, "Because I fell out of love with you a long time ago."

Beverley imagined herself snapping his neck. *Remember the program!* she thought, while standing to leave. "Here's your jacket back," she said and threw it to him.

"It's cold. Keep it for tonight," Kevin replied, his mouth still full of burger.

"I don't have that far to walk." Beverley struggled to keep her composure as she stormed out.

The wind cut through her sweater, and, although it wasn't snowing, the frozen ground crunched beneath the soles of her shoes. She tucked her hands deep into her jeans' pockets.

She didn't notice the fog that rose eerily from the nearby Cananee River, hovering inches off the ground. Nor did she pay any attention to the Northern Lights.

She needed to calm down, curfew or no curfew. The last thing she wanted to do was to vamp out in front of her new parents. She would be grounded forever! Not to mention having to face a stern lecture from Whittaker.

So she took the long way home, down the highway that cut past Sunset Park. When she reached the corner where the road turned down Devil's Highway, she decided to take a stroll through Sunset Park.

Most of the trees on the road towards the park were bare, making the town look like a cemetery. Beverley breathed a long trail of frozen breath, closed her eyes and wished away this one night. But when she opened her eyes things were just as before.

When she reached the bridge she stopped to watch the Cananee. She leaned on the wooden rails and listened to the water rush beneath her. She was still oblivious to the fog that was creeping onto the bridge.

"Beverley Longstraw?"

Beverley turned to face a stocky teen who blocked her path to the town.

"Yeah?"

The stranger stepped into the moonlight. His long hair was black, and his emerald eyes burned in the night. "You were adopted by the Longstraws one year ago."

"That didn't sound like a question."

The stranger stepped closer and growled, "Do you not know what I am?"

Beverley's face turned white, and her eyes widened. "Y . . . you! You found me!"

She turned to flee, but the hunter grabbed her long hair. He pulled her towards him, but she spun, landing a kick to the side of his head. He fell back, but was up in no time. He drew two graphite stakes holstered to his chest and lunged.

Beverley blocked the stake with her arm and punched the hunter. This time he didn't recoil, so she quickly pulled the stake from her arm and used it to stab him in the shoulder. He fell back but made no noise.

"I can beat you!" Beverley snarled.

But the hunter transformed. First, his nose and mouth grew into a canine face. Fur covered his clothes as they melted into his skin. His slightly crooked teeth grew long and sharp, and claws sprung from the tips of his fingers. He was the largest wolf that Beverley had ever seen.

"I don't remember how to use my powers," Beverley whispered.

She turned and fled towards Sunset Park, hoping to lose the wolf in the woods. She left the path and dove into the shadows of the trees and fog, which was now everywhere, obscuring fallen branches and overgrown roots. She ran wildly, when suddenly her foot caught and twisted on a root. She landed face first onto the ground.

Using the bushes around her for a hiding place, Beverley bit her lower lip to stop herself from crying. She cradled her foot, listening to the silence broken by the wolf's long howl. Beverley knew she had to get up and run if she ever wanted to see another sunrise.

Beverley forced herself up. The next howl came closer. And the next even closer. Until Beverley found herself face to face with the end of her life.

CHAPTER NINE

October 27th, 1989. Friday.

ith the bleachers folded out of the wall the school gym looked tiny. Jon sat in the center of the bleachers waiting for the assembly to begin. He expected it was a pep rally for the Wild Cats' new season and tried to ignore Nick and his crew who sat at the top, already hooting and hollering.

"Hey, Pyre," Lea said, standing next to him.

"Oh. Hi," he answered, shifting over to make room for her.

"I waited for you this morning," she said, sitting beside him. "You could have called to say you weren't picking me up."

"Sorry, I've just got a lot on my mind," he said. She sat so close to him that her bare arm pressed up against his. It always bugged him that their biceps were about the same size, but today he noticed that his muscles were almost twice hers.

"Have you been working out?" she asked.

"No," Jon answered quickly. If she noticed, had anyone else?

"What's wrong?"

"Nothing. Seriously," he lied.

"We know everything about each other, Pyre. What can't

you tell me?"

"Nothing!" Jon growled. He felt a pop in his ear, like he was on an airplane. He could hear every whisper around him, then suddenly his ears popped harder and the whispers silenced.

"Fine," she said, her voice flat and her lips curled. She stood up and began to make her way to where Nick was sitting.

"Great," Jon whispered. But at least this bought him some time from having to tell her about their parents. *What if she knows already?*

"Everyone not in the assembly please proceed to the gymnasium at once," the principal said over the intercom. The sound pierced Jon's ears as they popped once more, and he held his head to make the pain stop. No one else seemed affected except him. Again, as soon as it came, the super-hearing disappeared.

Jon looked around at the crowded gym and watched all the students and teachers, followed by a few stragglers, walk to their seats.

Mr. Jennings, the principal, walked to the center of the gym and grabbed the microphone. The cheering at the top of the bleachers amplified, with Nick shouting the loudest. Jon glanced behind him and watched Lea. She was sitting with them, but she wasn't cheering. When she caught him staring, he quickly turned around.

How am I going to tell her? He couldn't avoid her forever, not with two more years of school left. And he didn't want to. She was his best friend.

"Please settle down," Mr. Jennings said into the

microphone. "I have terrible news. Last night, Beverley Longstraw was killed in Sunset Park by a wolf."

Beverley Longstraw was killed. Jon stopped listening as the principal went on about available counseling and wildlife wardens who were hunting down the killer wolf. Instead, he remembered River Kitch and how he'd been asking about the Whittaker Orphans. Once at school, then at the gas station. This was too coincidental.

"In light of this tragedy, the Halloween dance is canceled. Counselors are available for anyone who needs one. Please proceed to your regular classes."

Everyone was whispering as they got up. Jon saw Paul rush out of the gym. Robert made his way to Karen, who was wandering away from her friends. They were the only three orphans left alive. Was there a killer targeting them? Did they know? Suddenly his ears popped again, and he heard Karen mutter to Robert, "Jon can't save us."

His hearing returned to normal too quickly for him to make out anything more. *This can't be happening,* Jon tried to convince himself. *The visions, the Dodgeball game . . . maybe if I concentrate.* Jon stared at the orphans, watched their lips move and imagined himself hearing them speak. At first he felt foolish, but suddenly he heard Karen say, "By the time he figures it out, we'll all be dead. I say we just tell him already!"

The students marched through the halls into their classes. Jon quickly ran to his locker, grabbed his coat and guitar and slipped into the janitor's closet.

The sun continued to shine as a fresh sheet of snow fell

on the prairies. A gentle breeze cooled Jon as he strummed a tune of his own making. The notes carried his thoughts away, until he swore he could see the music rising from his guitar like steam. He stopped playing and the notes disappeared. Then a pain hit his eyes and he shouted. Walls grew around him, cutting out the sunlight. The folding chair on which he sat became a velvet-covered dining room chair and a table appeared. Once again he saw the world through Liam's eyes, this time as a prisoner of the clan of vampyres.

"How am I going to both live and die?" Liam asked, no longer standing in the Great Hall but now sitting as one among many at a long dining table. Naztar sat at its head with Liam on his right. No one sat at the table's foot, yet there was a setting. Liam looked at his own setting: a silver plate rimmed with gold, a silver knife and a large silver-handled bowl. He looked into a chalice that perched innocently near his knife. It was filled with dark red wine as thick as blood.

"So many questions, Liam the Mighty. Be patient. First, we will feast."

"I thought vampyres didn't eat."

"You mortals are a strange lot." Naztar snapped his fingers, sending three demons near the foot of the table away in a puff of smoke. "It is true that we do not need food as substance to survive, but is that all dining is to you? A refueling of your body the same way you would refuel a lamp with oil?" He looked at Liam, with one eyebrow perked as if expecting an answer. When the three vampyres returned, they placed meat platters along the table. Naztar continued, "Substance is a minor part of eating. Feasting is an act of pleasure, and that is what being a vampyre is all about."

"You don't eat humans?"

"Tastes entirely too much like chicken."

Liam sighed loudly. "Then the whole drinking blood legend is false. All it means to be a vampyre is immortality."

"The blood legend is true. But it is for intoxication, not substance," Naztar said, his eyes glowing as brightly as the torches around him.

"And sunlight? Wooden stakes? An ax to the neck?"

Naztar laughed, his bellow resounding like a dragon's roar. The others along the table joined their Sage in his gaiety and the cavern echoed with the demonic chorus. Finally Naztar and the others quieted.

"I am not going to give you an education into vampyrism, Liam. Clear your mind. Feast and drink with us."

"I will do no such thing!" Liam's chair smashed to the ground as he stood up. "I am Liam the Mighty! If I am going to live then I demand to know why, and if I am to die then I shall do so as a man of honor."

Naztar rose, swooping up Liam's chalice and handing it to him all in one motion. The vampyre moved like a song played on an organ, a series of complicated movements performed so beautifully they appeared a simple thing. "You will die because we desire the blood that pumps in your veins, but you will live because you own something else we hunger for."

Liam took the chalice and picked up his chair. He sat again, feeling his bravado fade. "What?"

"Your family's wealth. We cannot enter a home uninvited, and your parents won't invite me no matter what trick I try. You will become a brother among us, and in return you will bring back the riches your family possesses." Naztar turned his back to the frightened boy, and pacing alongside the table, he took a strong swig from his own chalice. Naztar spun and walked quickly to stand behind Liam. Liam cringed as the vampyre gripped the back of his chair.

"As long as you can't enter my family's home," Liam hadn't meant to sound so hopeful, "you have to keep me alive."

A hand grabbed him, but it was Jon who felt it and not Liam. The presence of Jon's thoughts brought the room collapsing down around him, and Jon transformed back into himself. Snapping out of the dream, Jon breathed hard and saw Paul standing beside him.

"You okay?" Paul asked, wiping away the snow from the concrete so he could sit across from Jon.

"Look, I really need a personal moment right now," Jon said.

"Can I just listen to you play? I won't stay long, I promise."

Jon wanted to say no. He wasn't sure that he could play after that weird vision, but when Paul said, "A friend of mine just died. It would really help," he sighed. As he strummed "Here I Go Again" by Whitesnake, Paul began to sing. Jon's fingers felt shaky against the strings, but as

Paul sang on key he relaxed. They actually sounded good together. When Jon finished, he launched into "Don't Know What You Got" by Cinderella. Again, Paul sang the words.

"Hey, you have a great voice," Jon said.

"Thanks. And not just for the compliment. Thanks for letting me hang out here."

"No worries." Jon continued quietly strumming, having pushed the strange dream from his mind.

Paul smiled. "I really don't seem to be fitting in with the Whittaker crowd. I don't know if you've noticed, but they're all a bit weird."

"That's what most people think about me."

"You're a lot cooler than your rep would have people believe. So, the snow doesn't hurt your guitar?"

Jon shrugged. "Not really. It's cheap and doesn't really stay in tune. I'm saving up for an electric."

"Cool. What kind?"

"Probably a Casio DG-20 Digital Guitar."

"But that's not what you want. If you could have any guitar, what would it be?"

Jon shrugged.

"Come on, Jon. I won't laugh."

"A 1962 Sunburst Fender Stratocaster like Stevie Ray Vaughan."

"You know what? This town needs to hear your music. You want to play at a party I'm throwing tomorrow night?"

"You're throwing a party? Right after Beverley was . . ."

"She'd have wanted us to."

"What about your parents?"

"They're away. You have to come. Everyone will be there."

Jon kept plucking his strings. "Everyone will be at a party I'm invited to? I don't think so."

Paul laughed. "Jon, no one will turn down this party just because you're there. I know how parties work."

"I've never been to a party."

Paul grinned deviously. "Your chance to hang with the cool kids. I'll invite Karen."

Jon blushed. "It just doesn't sound like my thing."

"Because if Karen's there, Nick will be too?"

Jon stood and started packing up his instrument. "One of your friends just died last night," Jon said aloud while thinking, *and I have some really weird powers that keep popping up.*

"That's why we need a party. To keep spirits up and keep everyone safe in one place."

If everyone is at this party, maybe Kitch will be there. He needed answers that only Kitch could offer – such as who, exactly, he was and where he went during school hours. "Okay. I'll come, but I'll be late."

"The party won't even get started until well after dusk."

November 12, 1998.

Evil vampyres live for pleasure. They justify every action with the morality that if it feels good, then it must be good. I call that subjective morality.

After all, what feels good to a vampyre does not often feel good to humans. And what feels good to me, that is, the killing of vampyres, does not feel good to the evil blood suckers.

CHAPTER TEN

osmo buried his nose in the freshly fallen snow as he circled Jon. Jon's sneakers were soaked clean through, and he hadn't worn mitts. Yet even with his jacket open he didn't feel the cold.

"Weird," Jon whispered.

When he arrived at the After Dusk, he noticed the Honda Shadow parked in front. Judging from the lack of snow on it, the girl must have just arrived. Jon thought about the dead orphans, his strange powers and the weapons he'd seen in that girl's saddlebags. They all had one connection: Whittaker.

He stopped outside and saw that, although the lights inside were on, the shades were drawn. Cosmo nudged his hand to go. "I'm with you, buddy. Let's get out of here."

"You're not planning on bailing on us, are you?" Karen asked from behind him.

Jon spun around, and Cosmo slowly approached her, wagging his tail.

"Uh, I just wasn't sure there'd be anyone there. Y'know, because . . . uh . . ."

"Beverley died?" Karen walked past Cosmo without so much as offering a rub. She circled Jon, looking him up and down. He blushed and couldn't help but smile.

"Whittaker believes you have a place here at the After

Dusk. Me, I'm not so sure you do. At least not yet." Karen walked up to the house, but before she went in she turned to Jon, gesturing him to follow.

"Cosmo, wait out here," he said.

Inside, Paul was in the midst of carrying trays of stew to the table. Whittaker sat at the head of the dinner table. On his right sat the bleach-blond girl from the gas station. She was wearing the same tight, black leather pants and a tight tank top. She tapped her red nails on the table and smiled through equally red lips. Her hair fell loose over her shoulders.

"This is Jon," Whittaker said.

"We've met. I'm Fay," she said, while leaning back in her chair and kicking a foot onto the table. Whittaker glared at her and she sat back up.

The scent from the stew filled the room. Jon smiled and took a seat across from the newcomer.

He noticed a hard glare pass between Karen and Fay. When Paul placed a bowl of stew in front of Fay, he spilled some on her lap. He didn't apologize. Fay grabbed a napkin and cleaned herself up. Robert never looked at her. *Do they know about her weapons?* Jon wondered, as he picked at his food. A sharp pain suddenly pushed into his stomach, as if someone were giving him a needle.

"Fay is my granddaughter," Whittaker said, as if there had been a question asked of it.

"What brings you to Minitaw?" Jon asked, gulping down a mouthful of stew. The pain left and he felt a surge of energy ripple through him.

Fay smiled. "I go to a private school in Europe, but sometimes I have to come home to clean up my grandfather's house. Look around you, Jon. Doesn't this seem like a mess?"

"Maybe you should stay at your private school and let us clean this mess," Paul said, locking eyes with Fay.

"Now, now," Whittaker intervened, "let's not argue at the dinner table."

"I'm going for a walk," Paul said. Jon noticed that Paul scowled at Fay as he walked by her.

"Want some company?" Jon asked, swiveling in his chair to face Paul.

"He doesn't," Whittaker said before Paul could respond.

Paul stopped at the door. "Thanks anyway," he said, more to Whittaker than to Jon.

"Jon, I hear you're quite the musician!" Whittaker said quickly, after Paul shut the door.

"No one here wants to hear about my music." Jon turned back to the table and ate more of the stew. There was something weird happening to him again. It was that same sensation that took away his fears. As he swallowed, he started to want more and more stew. He stared at the other bowls and considered just taking them. *Who could stop me?*

"Do you want more?" Whittaker offered.

Jon did. He wanted it more than he'd wanted anything in his entire life. "No," he forced himself to say. Something was off here, and although Jon couldn't figure out what it was, he knew he had to escape. "In fact, why don't I just finish weeding the garden so I can end my time in this slave camp?"

Surprisingly, no one said anything. Robert just stood, raised his eyebrows to Karen, and together they cleared the table. Jon stood up, too, and instantly felt dizzy. He fell back into his chair, and everything around him flew into pieces like someone had overturned a chess board. *Not now!* Jon thought.

A beautifully decorated house came up around him. Expensive-looking tapestries hung from high ceilings, paintings in hand carved frames adorned the walls, and plush red carpet covered the floor. He was Liam again, this time sitting in a chair inside a dark room illuminated only by a shaft of light pouring through a narrow stained-glass window near the ceiling.

The Broadsword Fellows walked into the room, slowly approaching Liam.

"What is that smell?" Mike said, as he and Robert held their hands over their noses. They ran to the next room, while Paul crouched next to Liam.

"You've been missing for weeks, Liam. Where have you been?"

"I went into the cave as you dared me to," Liam said, without facing his friend. He stared off into the darkness, not stirring even when he heard Mike and Robert cry in terror.

"What have you done?" Paul asked.

"I found the vampyres."

Mike and Robert ran back into the room, just as Paul said, "Vampyres aren't real."

"He killed his parents! They're dead in the next room!" Mike shouted in horror.

Paul started to back away, but Liam grabbed his wrist. The two boys struggled, but Liam held fast as he said, "I have been bitten, and Naztar expects me to invite him to my home to take the riches."

"Vampires aren't real!" Paul yelled.

Liam stood and grabbed Paul by the throat. The other two boys ran for the doors, but now there were men standing outside. One of them, tall with a cloak that made him part of the night, shouted, "Invite me in!"

"What are you going to do to us?" Paul said, tears streaming down his cheeks.

"I will make you Brothers Among Us, and then you will help me to hide these riches from Naztar."

"Why?" Mike asked.

"Because this wealth is what keeps Naztar from killing me."

The tapestries, paintings and carpet swirled around Jon until he was once again back in the After Dusk. He breathed heavily, looking at each person in the room who was staring at him.

Do you know what's happening to me? Jon wondered. None of them said anything, as if waiting for him to speak. "I'm leaving!" Jon said and stood, nearly knocking over the entire table. He stormed to the door before anyone could stop him.

Once outside, he immediately called Cosmo. There was no answer.

"C'mon, Pyre. Let's make haste on those weeds," Karen said, joining him on the lawn.

"No, something's wrong. Cosmo never takes off," Jon said. "COSMO!"

"It's a dog. It wanders off. It'll wander back," Karen said, as she sat on the front steps.

Jon ignored her as he looked up and down the street. He heard a high-pitched yelp. "Cosmo!" he cried.

He cut through three yards before finally finding his dog. Cosmo was biting River Kitch on the wrist. Paul was on the grass. River, standing over him, had a stake in his hand.

Paul's clothes were torn and bloody. A stake was plunged deep into his shoulder. Cosmo seemed determined not to give River a second try. Jon had never seen his buddy so protective, and a feeling of pride swelled in him. But that feeling of pride instantly turned to fear as River lifted Cosmo off the ground and threw him against a tree so hard there was a loud crack. Cosmo landed on the ground, twisted in an unnatural way.

Power surged through Jon and he acted without thought. He dashed towards River, kicking him so that he flew several feet and landed in the snow. River recovered quickly, looked as though he considered fighting, but instead ran.

A part of Jon wanted to pursue River, but when he looked at Cosmo that desire faded away. His buddy lay bleeding on a bed of white snow. As Jon rushed to him, the whole world turned hazy. Tears welled in his eyes. He fell to his knees and crawled to Cosmo.

"No!" he repeated like a prayer. Cosmo's heart didn't beat. His chest didn't rise and fall. His tongue fell lifeless from his mouth.

Jon held his best friend tightly to his chest and cried.

Paul grunted as he pulled the stake out from his shoulder. He stood, dusting off his clothes, and said, "Cosmo saved my life. So did you."

"He can't be dead! I'll kill River for this!"

"Come on, Jon. I'll help you bury him."

Jon scooped the last of the dirt onto Cosmo's grave just before midnight. He had chosen a spot near the river, right where it entered Sunset Park. Cosmo had loved coming there to chase rabbits and fetch sticks. Jon's hands were dirty, his jeans were torn, and his T-shirt was cast off. But making the grave hadn't tired him out, nor had it exhausted his anger.

"I need a tombstone. Cosmo deserves a tombstone," Jon whispered, his jaw clenched.

"Use your anger to stop this killer. Do it for Cosmo," said Paul.

"I want to kill him," Jon admitted without a shred of remorse.

Paul picked up Jon's shirt and tossed it to him. "Don't underestimate River Kitch. He has power."

Jon caught his muddy shirt and pulled it on. Running his fingers through his long hair, he flexed his biceps and felt how muscular he'd become. "Maybe people should stop underestimating me."

Jon stared at Paul, deciding how much to trust him. That's when Jon noticed that the wound in Paul's shoulder, where River had stabbed him, had completely healed.

"River Kitch is not who he seems," Paul whispered.

"Neither are you," Jon said, picking up the shovel.

"No, I'm not." Paul looked away as if embarrassed. "I didn't come to Minitaw to go to Fillmore High. I came because I'm being hunted."

"By River Kitch."

"His real name is Rancour, Rancour of the Wulfsign." Paul walked up to Jon and placed his hands on his shoulders. "Your dog died saving me. You can honor his memory by protecting me."

CHAPTER ELEVEN
OCTOBER 28TH, 1989. SATURDAY.

he coffee was always perking before anyone was up. It ran on a timer, set for 9 a.m., so that when Jon's parents came down for breakfast they could have their instant pick-me-up.

As they finished off the carafe, Jon stomped down the stairs to the kitchen. His dad said nothing save for a grunt that might have been "Jon."

"Good-morning, honey," said his mom.

"Morning," he said, as he headed straight for the fridge. When he opened the door and took out the milk, his stomach rumbled. He took out the package of bacon and carton of eggs.

"You get three slices, Jon," his dad reminded him.

"Eddie, Jon has never eaten three slices in all his life. Two slices of bacon and one egg." She turned to Jon, and said, "Do you want me to make you breakfast?"

"No," Jon said, suddenly feeling like his stomach was on fire. He was hungry, starving, as if he hadn't eaten in a week, and found himself wanting to eat the bacon right out of the package. He turned on the stove and plopped the pan down on the burner. Opening the bacon package, he dumped all the meat into the pan.

His dad muttered something rude and left the room with

the paper. His mom moved in front of him and started flipping the bacon. "Let me," she said.

Jon gently pushed her aside and cracked six eggs over the bacon. "No, Mom. I got it."

"Okay," his mom said and sat on a chair. She looked around the room. "Where's Cosmo?"

Jon ignored his mom, scooping up the bacon and egg mixture into his mouth. His mom watched with disgust, opened her mouth as if to say something, but Jon spoke first.

"Cosmo's dead," he said before swallowing.

"What? How?"

Jon turned off the stove and walked out of the kitchen. His mom followed but stopped at the bottom of the stairs. He took them three at a time, then dashed into his room and shut the door. The mobs would be out today looking for a renegade wolf, when what they should be looking for is a renegade teen. River Kitch.

He'd become a part of something strange that was going on in Minitaw. First, his deal with Whittaker. Whittaker had enough orphans to fix up the After Dusk, so why recruit him? Second, his visions. Either there was some magical thing making him have them, or it was a tumor. It was time to stop ignoring them.

Whittaker, the visions, the orphans and River Kitch . . . they all had a connection. What was he being pulled into, and why him?

Jon stood in front of the mirror that hung above his dresser and examined his body. He had definitely filled out this past week. And, along with larger muscles, he had developed special powers. Only one person in this town seemed to be on his side, and only they could stop the murderer.

"We have a problem," Karen said, entering the After Dusk.

Whittaker, Fay, and Robert sat in a circle in the midst of a heated discussion.

"I have a truce with the council! They are to stay out of my business," Whittaker said.

"You *had* a truce when Rancour protected you. We won't let you get that power over us again," Fay said.

Karen pulled up a chair and sat down. "I think Paul is trying to get Jon to be his own personal Defender." The room fell silent as Karen continued, "He's befriended him. He's trying to take him away from us."

Whittaker leaned back in his chair and sighed. "Paul hasn't given himself completely to the program. We could wind up with a serious problem on our hands."

"One more reason why I'm not honoring the truce," Fay said. "Your experiment is detrimental to both the Council and this cult."

"That's hardly fair," Whittaker said.

Fay stood and walked to a desk where she'd thrown her saddlebags. "So speaketh Saint Whittaker. Pairing orphaned teens with clueless, innocent couples."

"Step off!" Karen growled and moved towards Fay. Robert stepped between them, although Fay hadn't reacted at all.

"Did anyone ever tell the parents what they were letting into their homes? Of course not. You didn't give them any more option than you gave Jon. Or me, for that matter!" Fay pulled out a handgun and checked the clip for bullets.

When no one spoke up, Fay continued, "How can any of you trust him? Whittaker is the reason we're all living this life!"

"He's also the only way out of it," Robert reasoned. "You can't deny it anymore. Not since he started aging sixty years ago!"

Whittaker came up behind Fay and placed his hands on her shoulders. "You have the choice now between darkness and light."

Fay shook him off and said, "Lucky for you I choose darkness, or there'd be no one to clean up this mess. I do those bad things you are so worried might damn you. If Paul is trying to take Jon for himself, then I'll find out why. Then after I kill Jon, I'll decide if I let Paul live."

They stared at one another as Fay holstered her gun, grabbed her jacket and walked out the door.

CHAPTER TWELVE

Jon played his guitar so loudly the sounds distorted, but he didn't care. He wanted the house to shake. This was a dare for his dad to come upstairs and ask him to stop. It took ten minutes before he heard banging on his door.

"What?" Jon shouted, as he gave the music a rest.

"Jon, honey, there's someone here to see you," Mom said.

"Who is it?" Jon asked, his voice softer for her than if it had been his dad.

"I don't know. I've never seen her before. She's pretty and has blond hair . . . can I come in?"

"No," he said quickly, as he unstrapped his guitar. *Could it be Fay?* he wondered. "Tell her I'll be right down."

A few minutes later, Jon stood at the top of the steps that led from his room to where the landing met the foyer. He hadn't bothered to run a comb through his hair, and he still had on his muddy shirt and torn jeans from last night. Sure enough, on the landing below, stood Fay Whittaker.

"Hey," Jon said, reaching the landing.

She smiled. "It seems we got off to a bad start, and I thought we could go for a ride and clear things up."

"I have to work, actually." Jon noticed that he hardly felt nervous. In fact, he hardly felt any emotion at all.

"Then I can give you a ride. Come on, my bike's outside."

The last thing Jon wanted was to get stuck hanging out with Commando Fay. *Maybe she knows about River?* That made sense. If she knew that River was killing the orphans and making the deaths look like wolf attacks, she wouldn't be hunting with weapons designed for an animal. She'd be hunting with exactly the kind of arms Jon had seen in her saddlebags. She could be an ally.

"Hey, Dad. I'm going to work now. Fay's giving me a ride."

His father, still in his bath robe, walked from the sunken living room just off the foyer. He was holding the newspaper tightly, opened to the sports section. He scowled at Jon, then looked Fay up and down, his eyes lingering on her chest.

"Who is this?"

"Fay Whittaker," Jon said.

"Fitzhenry, actually," Fay corrected.

"Of course it is," Jon muttered to himself.

"Is that your motorcycle outside?"

"Yes," Fay answered.

His dad's eyes narrowed. "Jon, you're not going anywhere. In fact, I think you'll be calling in sick today so you and I can have one hell of a discussion." He returned his attention to Fay and said, "You and Jon can have a play date some other time."

"I'm sure you wouldn't mind your son coming with me," Fay said, slowly and deeply.

His dad stared at her for a few long moments. He cocked his head a little, then looked as if he might nod off to sleep. Raising his head, but not averting his gaze, he said, "Of course. Go with her, Jon, and don't worry about our chat. I'm going to read the music page."

Jon watched Fay mouth every word his father had said.

"Okay . . ." Jon didn't know what to do. Fay was smiling now, her full red lips and dark-rimmed eyes bright against her otherwise alabaster skin.

"Are we ready?" she asked.

Jon had never ridden on a motorbike. He wasn't wearing a helmet or clothes thick enough to pad his skin should they have an accident. And, with the roads slick from frost, this was a definite possibility. His parka, T-shirt, and runners were fine for a brisk dog-walk but terrible for sliding across a pothole-ridden highway.

Yet it wasn't the fear of crashing that made his heart race. He pressed his chest against Fay's back, with nothing to hold onto but her waist. He'd never come this close to a girl before.

As the bike approached the gas station, Fay drove it into one of the parking stalls. The station always seemed different during the daylight hours and never in a good way. It looked like a shack right out of a horror movie, a place where the heroine would run to while being chased by the killer.

"Hey, kid. You can let go any time."

Jon released her and they climbed off together. "Sorry."

"Don't apologize. People will think you're weak."

"So you wanted to talk?" Jon started toward the front doors, fishing in his pocket for his keys.

"I hear you and Paul have become friends."

"Why are you in Minitaw?" Jon asked, opening the

door to the kiosk. This time he was taking control of the conversation.

Fay smiled and walked forward until she was pressed up against him. His heart started to quicken again, and he moved inside. Fay followed.

"You deserve the truth, Jon. Unlike Whittaker, I'm going to give it to you."

That certainly wasn't what Jon expected. "Good. About time."

"I am the daughter of Lord Fitzhenry. I was born in Nottingham, over a thousand years ago to a wealthy nobleman. I was coveted by many Lords."

"Whoa!" Jon said and put up his hands to stop her from continuing. *Is this truth time, or crazy time?* "You expect me to believe you're over a thousand years old?"

Fay, unfazed by his reaction, continued her story. "I was promised to a young knight, one whose reputation was approaching legendary. His name was Liam. Liam Whittaker."

Jon thought back to his visions, and to the name of the boy in them. "Liam is Whittaker's first name?" No one in town knew Whittaker's first name, which is why they called him Saint Whittaker. Somehow the visions had told him at least one thing that turned out to be true!

Fay said, "One night he went off with some friends, another of his many dares that would add to his reputation, but this time he didn't return."

"Naztar," Jon said, "they sent him to kill Naztar."

"The Broadsword Fellows sent him. Shortly after, his parents also disappeared and all their wealth. A year passed and my father decided it was time he found me another husband and promised me to a much older man whose wealth would make my family even richer. I ran away. I took my horse, Thunder, and we rode as fast and far as the night would allow. But the fog rolled in and darkness overcame us."

"How do you know about Liam? About Naztar?"

"You've been having visions, haven't you?" Fay gave him a moment to answer. When he didn't, she continued, "I knew Liam Whittaker long before he came to Minitaw. Long before Minitaw ever existed."

Fay pressed her hands against Jon's temples. Slowly, he met her eyes. They grabbed him, threw him off balance, and trees burst from the ground all around him. The gas station melted away into a fog that covered the woods, and out from the ground a horse appeared beneath Fay. She was now wearing a linen bell-sleeved tunic which was cinched around her waist with a belt. Her short hair was brown and jagged, as though it had been cut hastily with a knife. Jon melded into Fay, seeing what she saw. Feeling her teeth chatter almost as loudly as the clip clop of the horse's hooves.

Suddenly, howling sounded from within the mist.

Fay sat up straight on her horse, listening to the sounds. She closed her eyes. When she opened them, she was faced with six men and six hounds.

A seventh man stepped from the fog. He wore a long, midnight cape clasped at the neck by golden hooks and a collar that rose above his head like a mouth poised to howl. The mist parted into a dome around them, as if he'd commanded it to do so. Fay screamed.

The stranger threw his cape over one shoulder and crossed his arms, laughing until the echo from Fay's scream died.

"What would bring such a fair maiden out on a night such as this?" The stranger made an odd gesture with his hand, and the horse closed his eyes. Then the man bowed. "I am called Naztar."

Fay opened her mouth but shut it again when she saw the man's fangs. His cape opened like wings and he rose from the ground, hovering, waiting to feast.

"Child," he said, his voice soft, "you need not be afraid. I am going to release you from your bondage."

As Naztar enveloped her, Fay stopped shaking. He looked directly into her eyes and tilted his head to the right. She did the same. He slowly tilted his head to the left, and Fay mimicked his actions.

"You're mine, now," Naztar said, as he lowered his mouth to her skin.

He stopped as a voice cried, "Naztar! Find another to feast upon. Her life belongs to me."

Naztar let Fay go and spread his cape to create a barrier between the vampyres and the challenger. Fay caught herself from falling and peered through the fog to see who had claimed her.

"Liam," she whispered.

He stood gallant and proud. His complexion looked like that of a man who had died recently, but his long blond hair, brushed to the side, made him appear quite handsome. He was dressed in a well-tailored grey tunic, cotton breaches and tights. He stood with one foot propped upon a fallen tree and the other firmly upon the ground. He crossed his arms and pivoted his body as if ready to leap to her aid.

Liam glared at Naztar with an equally icy stare and did not flinch when the larger vampyre growled, "Liam, you have no right to this feast."

"I have not welcomed you to my home. You will give me this woman, or I will give you no more of *my* riches. Or perhaps you feel you can steal enough gold from the overtaxed villagers to bring you pleasure?"

"You will pay for this." Naztar's lips curled, and with a swish of his cloak, he disappeared. The wolves and vampyres followed, leaving Fay alone with Liam.

Fay's horse, still paralysed from Naztar's spell, breathed hard and fast. Liam reached out and caressed the steed, meeting the animal eye to eye.

"Sleep, stallion. Sleep and dream of pleasant pastures."

The horse's eyes closed, and gently the beast collapsed onto the damp sod, rolling onto its side. Liam turned to Fay.

"We were meant to be together, Fay. Come to me and I will give you Forever."

She approached him with hesitant steps. When she was near enough, he reached out with both hands and she took them, leaning on him for support. He embraced her tightly. With a gentle stroke of his hand, he brushed back her long hair while caressing her spine with his other.

"Are you going to turn me?" Fay whispered to Liam.

"Not yet," he whispered in return. He brushed his lips over hers, while continuing the gentle caress of her spine. "First we find Pleasure."

The vision turned blurry, and Jon started to pull away from it. This feeling was like trying to struggle out of a deep slumber. His body turned cold and his heart stopped beating. Suddenly the spell shattered and Jon regained control over his words. He glared at Fay. "Turn around and leave!"

She smiled, unfazed by his reaction. "Death is nothing to be afraid of, Jon."

He calmed his breathing and the coldness left him. His head started to spin and he leaned against the counter for support. "What the hell is happening to me?"

"It's time for you to make a decision. Leave the After Dusk and never return, or I'll do what I came to do," Fay said, reaching into her jacket.

Before Jon could answer, a horn from outside beeped and a car door shut. Fay turned and looked out the glass door to see that a family of four in their camper van had pulled up to the pumps. The two children got out with their mom and started for the kiosk.

Fay smiled, winked and turned to leave. Stopping in the doorway, she glanced back once, her eyes filled with hunger.

"Have a good day at work," she said. "I'll see you later."

"Y . . . yeah," he stammered.

Jon grabbed his work coat and headed outside to the pump. *Was she reaching for a gun?* he wondered as Fay took off down the highway. Jon wanted, he needed, to tell someone about what was happening. He needed to talk to someone not connected to Whittaker.

November 14, 1998.

The thing with vampyres is that they can become
whatever they need to be to get whatever they
need to get. I don't know if that means they can
shape-shift into wolves or bats, but I do know that
they can turn from the meanest personality to your
sweetest desire.

But then who among us can claim that we don't
change our personality to attain what we desire?

CHAPTER THIRTEEN

he phone rang a third time as Lea scrambled with her keys in the lock. She rushed inside, threw her bag onto the table and grabbed the receiver. "Hello?"

"Hey, it's Jon."

Lea tried to regain her composure. "Oh. What do you want?"

There was a long pause before Jon said, "I need to talk to you. Can you stop by the gas station?"

He sounded sad, and she wished she could just forgive him and forget that they had ever fought. But he'd really hurt her, so she said, "I can't. I was just going to phone Nick and see if he'd change the oil in my Jeep." It wasn't true, but since Jon usually did it for her, she knew this would bother him.

"I'll change the oil while we talk. Come on, Lea. Please?"

"Fine. I'll be right there."

It only took fifteen minutes to get from Lea's to the gas station, but Jon waited for nearly three quarters of an hour before he saw the Jeep.

"Hi, Pyre," she called out the window.

"Took you long enough," he said, as he opened the garage door and guided her onto the ramps. Once the engine was off and the parking brake secure, Jon lay back on a dolly and rolled under the engine.

Lea got out of the Jeep and wandered over to the ghetto blaster. As she examined a stack of tapes, she asked, "What's so important, anyway?"

Jon grunted as he loosened the oil pan nut. "I got a ride from this girl who showed up at my house."

"Girl? Who was she?"

"No one from around here."

"At the assembly, Nick asked me to a party."

Jon stopped working on the Jeep, realizing she had changed the subject. "You're going out with Nick?"

"I didn't say I was going out with him. So, if she's not from around here, where's she from?"

"Whittaker's granddaughter, so she says. I don't know. Are you going out with him?"

"It's just a party. Why, are you jealous?"

"I'm not jealous," he said. *Am I?*

"Maybe I will go to the party." Her voice sounded cold.

"Whatever. You know the guy's only after girls for one thing."

"You don't think he might like me for myself?"

"I'm just saying he has a reputation for moving fast. I don't have to be jealous to not want you to get hurt."

Was she mad at him? Jon rolled out from under the Jeep. Her face was red and she held her arms close against her chest. He grabbed a hose from the nearby wall and put the nozzle into the crankcase. As the motor whirred and the oil filled, both Jon and Lea let the silence between them fill with music.

"Are we done?" Lea asked, after Jon put the nozzle back on the wall and closed the hood.

"I guess we are." Lea got back into her Jeep. He wanted to tell her about his dad and her mom. He even wanted to tell her about the deal he'd made with Whittaker, about Fay and the weapons she carried around and about River Kitch. But she was so mad that he couldn't. But he did say, "Cosmo died, by the way."

Lea had already started to drive off, leaving Jon to wonder whether she'd heard him or not.

"So, you're actually going to date Lea?" Bob asked.

"Yeah," Nick replied.

The sun was setting and the wind was picking up, sending ripples across the pond in the park. The pond was an ideal place to hang out, far enough from town where no adults would bother them. Nick had left the side door to his van open and music blared from inside. While most of the gang sat around a picnic table playing cards and drinking beer, Tim, Bob and Nick threw around a football. It was a typical weekend gathering.

"Lea is a princess. I can't believe you made us let her join cheerleading," Karen said as she took a swig from her bottle.

"Kick her out when I'm done with her. Whatever," Nick said, hurtling the football to Tim.

"I'm not that cold," Karen answered, ignoring her friends' laughter.

"Then deal with having her on your squad." Nick said.

"You're so mean . . ." Sandra said with a smile.

Karen interrupted, "Maybe Lea'll surprise us all and give Nick the big 'no.'"

Nick glared at her. "Right. And maybe pigs will fly. I'll bag her. Trust me," he growled.

CHAPTER FOURTEEN

After work Jon spent most of the afternoon sitting on the couch with his guitar. He missed having Cosmo lying beside him. He even missed the scolding he'd get from his mom for letting the dog onto the couch. Squeezing his arms tight against his chest, he tried to force out the heartache. His shirt felt snug against his skin. His biceps and pecs had grown even larger.

Then it happened again. The ceiling above him blew away and the walls around him fell flat against the ground. The walls returned, old and cracked, and formed an old cabin. Jon, as Liam, stood outside wearing a red silken tunic and bright blue breaches.

"Come, Peter. Invite me in," Fay said, standing outside a window nearby.

"Nay, I shan't. Begone and leave me be," came a voice from within the cabin.

"Do you have such little faith in your God? Will He not protect you, should you let us in?" Liam shouted, as he moved beside Fay at the window.

Liam saw Peter reach to a nearby table to scoop up a leather-bound book with black lettering that read, "The Bible."

"It is not right to test God," Peter said matter-of-factly, opening the book. "It is He who tests us."

"Are you afraid He will fail a test?" Liam answered, amused by Peter's strange devotion.

Peter laughed and closed the book. Walking to the window, he said, "My pride is not toyed with so easily. Go find a child to play with."

Seeing that Peter had come to look outside, Liam snapped his fingers and Fay held up a child they'd kidnapped earlier. The boy was no more than five with sandy hair and blue eyes that could melt a winter away.

"You beast! How could you?" Peter cried.

"Give your life for the child and we won't. Do you believe in Eternity? Invite me in."

Peter bowed his head. "You will release the child if I do?"

"Aye, that we will. Invite me in, and invite Fay to you."

"That I do, damn thee!"

The wooden doors to the cabin slowly creaked as the rusted hinges moved. Liam walked to Peter, who put his Bible back onto the table. Liam said, "You best go outside, Peter. It would be a shame if Fay killed the child in hunger."

Peter tried speaking but no words came. Silently, he walked outside and stood before Fay. Liam turned to watch.

"Let the child go," Peter said, before fear stole away the last of his voice.

"As you wish, Master." Fay released the child, whose eyes turned ablaze. Suddenly the child's innocent mouth filled with fangs, and his tiny nails turned into sinewy claws. The child leaped at Peter, sinking his teeth into Peter's neck.

The only sound that night louder than the hunted screams was the laughter from the vampyress. Liam ignored the screams and laughter from outside. He looked around the cabin, knocking over the few knick-knacks. "A wasted life is one so impoverished," he said.

A dog slumbered by the fire, obviously deaf to his master's cries for help. Liam took the chair and sat, looking at the black book that Peter had left on the table. He touched it and instantly his finger burst into flame. Liam recoiled from the burn, snuffing out the flame on his tunic. The book was not at all harmed.

"There is no God. There is only the Pleasure!" Liam whispered.

Liam touched the book again, recoiling from another burn.

"There is power in this," he whispered. "Maybe it is power I can use against Naztar!" Scooping it into his satchel, he scorched his hand but did not react to the pain.

"Fay!" he called. "We must return. It will be dawn soon."

The phone rang, snapping Jon from the trance. The cabin fell away, and he was once again in his living room, lying on the couch. His head raced and pounded, but he managed to reach for the receiver.

"Hey, Pyre," Lea said. Her voice was soft. "My mom just told me about Cosmo."

"I buried him yesterday," Jon said, still a bit lost in the trance. "There are a lot of weird things going on."

"That's why you wanted to talk?"

"Partly. Can we get together later?"

There was a pause. "No. Nick's invited me to a party, and I said I'd go."

"You're actually going out with that jerk?"

"Yes. And he's not such a jerk."

Jon considered telling her about the fight, but he knew she wouldn't believe him. "Fine. Whatever. But that's not until tonight."

"Why don't you come now?" Lea asked.

"Thanks," Jon said before hanging up the phone. Just then his dad walked in.

"Father," he said in a way that he knew would bug him.

"Why are you being such a jerk?"

"I'm being a jerk? You're the one having an affair!"

"Shhh! Your mom's in the next room! You let this get out, and you'll only hurt her."

"No, Dad. Whether or not this gets out, whether or not you understand this, you've already hurt her." Jon got up and stood in the doorway. "And whether or not you care, you've hurt me, too."

With that Jon walked out.

Jon banged on Lea's door. Ms. Black opened it, her smile clearly forced.

"Hi, Jon."

"Is Lea here?" Jon glared at her. What a crappy week.

"I heard about Cosmo. You must be heartbroken," Ms. Black said. She moved towards him as if to hug him. He backed away. Jon fully appreciated why the women in Minitaw didn't trust her.

"Are you going to let me talk to Lea?"

She walked out and shut the door behind her. "Should we talk first?"

"What's going on?" Lea asked, opening the door. "Jon,

Mom, why are you guys outside?"

Jon ignored the glower from Ms. Black. "Let's take a ride, Lea," he said.

Lea followed Jon to the Jeep. They climbed in without saying anything. Bananarama's "Cruel Summer" blared from the speakers when she turned on the engine. She slipped the vehicle into gear and pulled out onto the street.

"Are you okay? I'm so sorry about Cosmo," she said softly, driving towards the highway.

"Something weird is going on, Lea." Jon didn't know where to start. His deal with Whittaker, the visions, the powers, Fay, or River? Suddenly, the affair didn't seem so important.

"Don't try to talk me out of going to the party with Nick, okay?"

That wasn't what he wanted to talk to her about, yet he still muttered, "The guy treats me like crap and now you're going out with him."

"It's not open for discussion."

"Fine," he said, as she stopped at a red light. Why had he even bothered? She wasn't open to discussing anything. He hopped out of the Jeep. "Have fun at the party."

She looked at him icily, but this time only for a second. "I thought you needed to talk."

"Say hi to Nick for me," he said, slamming the door before she sped off.

"Damn!" Jon said, as his anger rose and the coldness returned. This time he would take his powers to their source: Whittaker.

CHAPTER FIFTEEN

Fay's bike was parked outside the After Dusk. Jon crept up to the kitchen window, listened but heard nothing. He crept toward the living-room windows and heard Fay's voice through a crack in an uneven board.

"I told him the truth!"

"He wasn't ready for it, Fay," Whittaker pleaded.

"You've done this before. You trained Rancour to hunt your enemies, thinking you could control him. You were wrong then, just as you are wrong now."

"We need him, Fay."

"For what? Just who, exactly, are your enemies? After Rancour, will you send him after us?" Fay sounded angry.

"So, this is what this is about. The Council wants to keep its control."

"You will expose us all if you take this boy from his family."

"No one in this town will miss him. Especially his family."

"Then neither will you . . ." Fay's voice faded, as if she had walked out of the room.

Jon's heart raced as he realized they were talking about him. Whittaker was training him? Just like he'd trained Rancour? *That must be why he's killing the orphans . . . some sort of revenge,* thought Jon.

What did Paul know about this? Was Paul in on Whittaker's plans? Was Karen? Whatever was going on, it was very odd, and the last thing he wanted was to wind up a resident of someone's freezer.

Fay stormed out from the After Dusk. She didn't see Jon as she got on her bike and sped away down the street. This was his chance to find out from Whittaker what was going on. Jon walked to the door, wishing he had Cosmo with him, and bashed his fists on it. Whittaker answered and smiled.

"Jon. You've come to paint . . . "

"Stop it, Mr. Whittaker. I want the truth from you."

"Are you saying you're ready and that you wish it of your own will?"

"Yeah, whatever. Just tell me!"

Whittaker led Jon inside, and the two of them sat at the kitchen table. Stew was cooking in the other room, and Jon could smell it. The scent was incredible, sending ripples over Jon's skin and making him drool.

"Do you want some supper?" Whittaker asked.

"Look, just tell me what's going on," Jon said in a whisper, forcing himself to ignore the aroma.

"I will give you the answers you seek, but the story shall be long. Do you want dinner while I tell it?"

"Yeah, okay," Jon said. But Whittaker hadn't waited for Jon's reply. He'd already disappeared into the kitchen and returned with a large bowl of steaming hot stew. The aroma untied the knots in Jon's stomach as he immediately scooped it into his mouth. He swallowed without chewing, and even when he choked, he didn't stop.

Whittaker sat again and said, "Slow down, Jon. Enjoy this. You never know what meal will be your last."

"Give me more!" Jon's heart started to race.

"Not until I have told you my story," Whittaker said. "Have you been having strange visions?"

"Yes," Jon said. Whittaker lunged across the table and grabbed him by the temples. The table turned into a bureau. The wooden walls changed to stone. The electric lights became fiery candles. Whittaker disappeared and so did the stew. Jon was sitting at the bureau, staring at a book, no longer himself. He was Liam.

Liam was hunched over a book in pensive admiration. Fay hummed lullabies from childhood as she wandered about their home dusting all the golden trinkets.

"It's a New Moon! Our power is at peak!" Fay sang from behind him, twirling like a dancer, unable to control her excitement. She grabbed a small golden statue and sat on the bed to admire it.

"That must be an interesting book. You've been lost in it forever."

"Lost," Liam repeated softly, as he turned in his chair to look at her. "I have found my Shepherd. I am lost no more."

"Then let me have him first, so we can both get drunk on his life." She rose, leaving the statue on the bed, and straddled the chair so that she sat upon his lap. "Or we could find Pleasure together and drunkenness later."

Liam pushed her from him before their lips met,

knocking her to the floor. "Fay! It isn't right, this life we lead."

"Isn't right? What say you? We are married!"

"Are we? We were married by Naztar, and what right does he have to join us as man and wife?"

Fay rose from the floor, and reaching for the book, she said, "What madness have you found in . . . ouch!" She screamed and recoiled from the book, her fingertips smoking.

"Is it madness, Fay? If it is, then why does it burn you when no other book does? Why is it we cannot harm those with faith?"

"Do not say such things!"

"I will, Fay. I will beg his forgiveness for the wrongs I have done." He turned from her and added softly, "For the wrongs I have done you."

"We are, by nature, what evil is! There is no amount of good that can replace the evil you've done."

"For it is by grace you have been saved, through faith . . . and this not from yourselves, it is the gift of God . . . not by works, so that no one can boast."

"If Naztar hears you speak this madness he will take away your Forever." She fell to her knees, her eyes wet with moisture.

"Forever? What is that compared to Eternity? Go if you want to get drunk, but I am staying in again. I will speak to Him tonight. And beg His forgiveness."

"Then tonight you will die, Liam. Treasure or no treasure, Naztar will kill you."

Suddenly the bureau morphed back into a table, and the stone walls turned into wooden panels. Jon opened his eyes and saw that Whittaker had released him.

"Fay was telling me the truth! You can't . . . be . . ."

"A vampyre," Whittaker finished, as he took away Jon's empty bowl. Before returning to the kitchen, he said, "I can be."

Jon stood and slammed a fist on the table. "YOU CAN'T!"

"You can still walk away, Jon. Leave the After Dusk and never return, and you will go back to the way you were."

A part of him wanted to rip the old man apart. "I'm leaving," he said in a voice that warned Whittaker not to stop him.

"Then we will all die. Paul, Robert, Karen, and I. And any vampyres who wish to leave their evil lives will have nowhere to go."

"That's not my fault."

"It is if you have the means to stop it. Will you at least listen to the rest of my story?"

"Fine," Jon said, allowing Whittaker to place his hands over his eyes. The warm air turned cold, and the crackling of the wood stove became the chirping of sparrows. Whittaker's hands turned into cloth pulled tightly over Jon's eyes. When Jon tried to pull the cloth away, he found that his hands were tied behind his back.

"If you wish to kill me, Naztar, then do so!" came the voice of Liam from Jon's lips.

The cloth was ripped from his head, and Jon saw trees all around him. He was on his knees; it was dark, and the narrow path that wound its way through the woods was barely visible in the dim moonlight. Blood dripped from his nose, and his face hurt as if he had just been beaten. Naztar stood before him with Fay at his side.

"If your faith is so strong, then why not use it to defeat me?" Naztar taunted.

Liam thought back to Peter in the cabin. He recalled how he had tormented the poor man, daring him in the same way that Naztar now dared him.

"It is not my place to test God," Liam choked. "My soul is saved. Kill me if you will."

"No. That task I leave for your lover. Will you kill her to save yourself?"

"No," Liam whispered.

Naztar grabbed Liam by the hair and forced him to look up. He held his fist above Liam's face and said, "Beg for your life, and perhaps I shall spare it."

"Liar! But this at least is truth: kill me, and your riches will end," Liam said.

Naztar replied, "You took Fay as your wife. Whether you are alive or dead she can invite me inside, and I can take all your wealth."

Naztar handed Fay the stake, forcing her to take it though her hand trembled so much she nearly dropped it. She looked softly at Liam, then pleadingly at Naztar.

"Time for you to choose sides, Fay!" Naztar growled. Before she could choose, a wolf bounded from the woods and knocked her to the ground.

The wolf growled, "This man shall not die today," and then transformed into a man, clad in leather armour with a long Claymore sword strapped to his back. He looked exactly like River Kitch.

Naztar faced him and bellowed, "Who are you that has come to die?"

"Challenge me and learn," the werewolf said and drew the Claymore.

"Begone foolish one, or you shall take this *man's* place."

The werewolf stood between Naztar and Liam. "Challenge me and I will show you what kind of man I am!"

"A brave one I see," Naztar smiled. "Perhaps I shall battle you."

"Then do so!" Rancour slammed the sword into the earth, as if to show that he didn't need it to fight a vampyre.

"Before I kill you, tell me why you wish to save this man."

"A vampyre killed my soul-mate. I hunt him and any other whose path I cross!"

Naztar laughed so loudly that tears came to his eyes. "You would save this man because you abhor my kind?"

"Aye, that is why. Now have at you!"

"Nay, werewolf. I shall leave in peace so that you might see what it is you have saved." Naztar opened his cape and disappeared in a puff of smoke and the girl, shooting the man on the ground a pleading glance, disappeared along with him.

The werewolf untied Liam. "You are met well, friend. Do not be afraid. I won't harm you."

Liam stood and offered his hand. "I thank you for your

kindness."

The werewolf didn't take the hand offered. Before turning to leave, he said, "A kindness would have been to slay the beast. They'll return for you."

"Then why did you not slay them?"

"Because I cannot kill vampyres."

"You are one of faith?"

"No. I am one who lacks knowledge. I did not kill because I do not know how." The werewolf turned and started to walk down the path. He stopped only when Liam said, "I can teach you about vampyres."

"Whatever knowledge you have of vampyres is false."

Liam spread his cape wide and flew into the air. Hovering above the werewolf he said, "Do not assume to know a man when you have only just met him."

"Mockery!" the werewolf shouted, shifting back into the wolf.

Liam returned to the ground. "I will not challenge you. I have lived an evil life for long enough. If you will not befriend me, then begone!"

Liam turned to leave but stopped when the werewolf turned back into a human and shouted, "Wait! Please teach me how to triumph over one of you."

"What are you called, friend?"

"Rancour. Rancour of the Wulfsign."

The vision started to collapse, and as Jon came out of it, he heard Whittaker saying, "Fay betrayed me after I reformed. She invited Naztar into the cave and together they chose to kill me. So I trained Rancour, a werewolf, to protect me. I thought he would reform as well and see that not all vampyres are evil. Instead, he used my training for his own purpose: to kill all vampyres. The bad and the good."

"Those who followed Naztar and those who followed you," Jon said, his head spinning from all the information.

"Yes. It was only a matter of time before he came after me. Now do you understand why I had to change you?"

"No," Jon said. Even with Whittaker's story, his world no longer made any sense. Vampyres, werewolves, and . . . what the hell was he, exactly? "I'm leaving. Don't try to follow."

Jon pushed his chair away from the table and waited for Whittaker to say something. Common sense told him that everything happening around him was a lie, that there had to be some sort of trick. But this wasn't a dream. This was real life. Whittaker picked up the dirty bowl and took it into the kitchen. Jon stood, grabbed his jacket and left the After Dusk.

Outside the wind had picked up and the cold nipped his nose. Yet he knew that he wasn't feeling the frozen night air the way he should. *Who can help me?* he wondered as he headed down the highway towards Icy Shakes' parking lot. When he found himself standing outside the restaurant, engulfed in the aroma of frying burgers, he heard Fay's motorcycle pull up from behind.

"Pretty trippy, huh?" Fay asked.

"None of this can be real," he whispered.

"It's real, Jon. What Whittaker is, and what I am. And what I have to do."

CHAPTER SIXTEEN

Lea stood in a corner of the house, hugging her chest and staring at her shoes — black heels to go with her Cat Woman costume. At home she had been worried that no one would like her outfit, but now she was worried because no one else was in costume.

Sandra walked by with Bob. "Lame," they whispered together.

All Lea could do was try not to cry.

She stood on the edge of what had become the dance floor. In the basement a group of boys were shooting pool, and in the upstairs rooms . . . Lea didn't even want to think about what was going on in those rooms. She was no longer sure why she had come.

She wondered where Pyre was and what it was that he'd wanted to tell her. Why was he being so secretive? Who was that girl who had given him a ride?

"Hey, Lea," Karen said. She had a drink in one hand and a cigarette in the other. "Nice outfit. Me-ow!"

Lea looked up from the floor and glared at Karen.

"You do that well," Karen said.

"What?" Lea said with a little more confidence.

"The *cold bitch* routine. I'm surprised we've never hung out before."

Lea glared at her again.

"I was just kidding. Peace treaty? If you're going to be a cheerleader, you'll have to get used to my teasing."

"Bullying is more like it."

Karen smiled. "That's it! Show a spine!"

Lea sighed and looked around. Wasn't Nick supposed to be here?

"Nick won't come until later." Karen answered her unspoken thoughts. "What grade are you in?"

"Grade 11. Same as you." When Karen didn't seem convinced, Lea added, "We're in some of the same classes."

"Wow. I guess we won't be strangers anymore." Karen stared at her for a moment, then handed her the drink she was carrying. "Have this. I'll go get another."

Lea took a sip of the drink and nearly choked. "What – what is it?"

Karen laughed. "Welcome to the cool kids, honey."

"Whose house is this?"

"Paul's," Karen answered. "Want me to show you around?"

"I think I'm okay just staying here."

"Suit yourself, Wallflower. But I didn't come to this party to hide."

Karen suddenly pushed into the crowd that had started dancing. Lea considered following, but Nick came up from behind.

"Hey. Glad you came," he said, brushing up beside her.

Lea smiled and forgot about Karen and Pyre. "I thought it was a costume party."

"Maybe everyone else knew you'd outdo them."

Lea laughed and took a sip of her drink. It suddenly didn't matter where Pyre was or who wore what to this party. She was just glad that Nick had turned out to be a cool guy.

CHAPTER SEVENTEEN

J on didn't want to be alone with Fay, the psycho armed-to-the-teeth lover of the man who trained the serial killer at large. Before she did anything, he quickly asked, "Why me?"

Fay stood in front of the restaurant. "I'd go crazy in this isolated prison," she mumbled, looking at herself in the window.

She tucked her fists into her coat pockets. Jon noticed that while her reflection in the window was ghost-like, his reflection was strong. She stepped away from the glass.

"You really are a vampyre?"

"I'll give you one last chance to walk away. Go back home. Forget what you saw last night."

"If I do, I let everyone die." Jon couldn't stop his hands from shaking. He tucked them into his coat pockets, then took a step towards the glass.

"If you don't, you'll die."

"Why kill me? Why not go after River?"

"*Rancour* isn't my contract. There's someone else on him, and it isn't my place to interfere. You, Jonathan Pyre, are my contract."

"Why?"

"Because you're becoming a Defender. Whittaker gave you his blood, lots of it, and now you've begun to change."

"He never bit me," Jon said quickly, his eyes wide.

"No, but you ate his stew. Whittaker used that stew to feed you boiled vampyre blood."

"What? Why?"

"In hopes the blood would change you without turning you. Whittaker wants you to fight his enemies."

"Like River."

"And probably us."

Jon shook his head. "I just want things to go back to the way they were."

"Then go home."

Jon pushed her away. "It's not that simple. I can't just let River kill more people."

He stormed off, but Fay appeared in front of him. "It isn't people he's killing. You have a clear conscience, and if you leave Minitaw tonight I'll let you live."

There was a snap in Jon's mind as his fist landed straight in Fay's face. She stumbled backwards but recovered quickly. Jon didn't even see her heel smack his temple, but he certainly felt it as he flew to the ground. A group of people ran out from Icy Shakes, one of them yelling, "What's going on?"

"Nothing." Fay glared at Jon before walking away.

The crowd waited for Jon to say something. He felt his forehead, but there was no blood or scar. Then he listened, focusing his hearing on the buzzing from the street lamps, the sound of meat frying within the restaurant and a song, "Sweet Dreams Are Made of This," playing down the street. He heard Fay's footsteps walking towards the music.

Jon hurried in the same direction, down Pike Avenue. As

he neared Paul's house, he came across Lea's Jeep. She was definitely at the party.

He quickened his pace, cutting across the street. Music blared from the house's open windows. Out on the lawn, teens milled in circles drinking and laughing. Couples clustered on the front steps, talking so loudly that it was a wonder the cops hadn't busted the place. Every one of them went silent as Jon took to the steps.

It was smoky inside and dense with the pungent smell of sweat. Jon wrinkled his nose and considered leaving. But he had to find Paul and find out what he knew.

"The man of the hour has come," Paul said, as he weaved his way through the crowd.

"Yeah. Listen. We have to talk."

Paul laughed. "If you're worried about Minitaw's finest, then Frankie says relax. A simple contribution to their retirement fund, and we have a 'get out of jail free' card."

Jon paused. Then he grabbed Paul and slammed him against the wall. The hall filled with on-lookers.

"How much do you know?" Jon growled.

"You figured it out." Paul sounded relieved. "Please, Jon. You know I'm on your side."

"You're lying!" Jon held his fist back as if to punch him.

"I'm not! Why do you think I never fit in with the Whittaker Orphans?" Paul shouted back. Jon started to relax his grip. "I was always on your side."

"What do I do now?"

"Tonight, you play one heck of a concert. We can figure out the tougher questions tomorrow. Come on. I made a space for you to play in the living room. Your audience awaits, Jon."

"I don't have my guitar."

Paul slapped Jon's back. "No worries. Follow me."

Taking a deep breath, Jon wove his way through the crowd after Paul.

"Over here," Paul shouted over the noise. They walked into the living room where a crowd was dancing. Jon looked at the space where Paul had made a stage. On each side were two speakers as tall as him and an amp connected to a 1962 Sunburst Fender Stratocaster. Jon picked it up and caressed the Brazilian rosewood veneer fingerboard, gently plucking the strings. "This is fretted with Dunlop 6100 Jumbo fretwire! It's like the one Stevie Ray Vaughan plays," Jon said in awe.

"It's yours. All for you," Paul assured him.

Jon cleared his throat and felt his fingers begin to shake. He remembered trying to play for Nick when he was scared and how terrible he'd sounded. "I don't think I can do this," he said.

"Maybe Jon can't," Paul said as he opened a nearby closet and reached inside. He pulled out a brown leather jacket and a black bolero hat. "But I bet Pyre can!"

Jon took the jacket and hat. "I can't switch identities just like that."

"It's what rock stars do. Put it on. Try it."

Jon put on the jacket and hat. He walked to the stage, picked up the guitar and caught a glimpse of himself in the window. Looking over his shoulder, he pulled the hat's brim low over his eyes and said, "Let's do this!"

Lea watched Jon take the stage and pick up the electric guitar. He was dressed in a new leather jacket and black hat. She kept a discreet eye on Jon as she pushed herself a little closer to Nick, just in case Jon spied her.

Nick put his arm around her and leaned in closer. Ugh. Beer breath. Lea pretended to be fascinated by Nick's breakdown of last week's game against Mattheson High, and how they kicked the big city kids' butts.

The cheerleaders, as they danced to New Order's "Dreams Never End," started whispering and giggling as they noticed Jon. "Is he new?" one cheerleader asked.

"Nope," Karen answered loudly, her eyes never leaving Jon's biceps. "He's just become all he can be."

Lea felt Nick nudge her, obviously sensing that he was losing her interest.

Paul hit stop on the tape deck, and the crowd cursed.

"Friends, thank-you for coming to my home." As Paul spoke, everyone fell silent. "Unlike the adults who have allowed a few wolf attacks to scare them into locking their doors, my doors are open! Tonight we party, not because we don't understand the danger that lurks outside, but because we refuse to let it control our destinies! Lift your glasses to the ones the wolf has taken. To Mike! To Beverley!"

Everyone cheered. Even Nick held up a glass, but Lea suspected that was more to bring the attention back to himself. He was such a typical point guard! As Paul went on, talking about Fillmore High's great basketball team, Lea noticed Jon look at her. She'd hung her hair loose and teased it the way he liked and had on the red lipstick that he once said made her look like a model. Maybe if Jon saw someone else treating her as a girlfriend, he might see her the same way. She made sure to stand close to Nick, holding her drink confidently.

". . . for your pleasure I bring you, Pyre!" Paul said as he stepped away. Jon didn't seem to realize that he was on. Lea dared a glance, but he was staring at Karen who mouthed, "PLAY!"

Jon strummed his guitar but stayed rigid like a statue. Slowly, the chords came more easily, and Lea watched him as he kept his eyes on Karen. The chords turned into a melody. He plucked slowly and rhythmically, and after awhile he began to sing. He sang about loneliness, being on the fringe, living life vicariously through others. Lea wished he was playing that song for her, and her alone. When he finished the crowd stared at him, until someone yelled, "Play something we can dance to, you nerd!"

Everyone laughed and Jon froze. But not for long. Suddenly, he jumped like the stage was on fire and he began to rock out "Life by the Drop." No one danced. They just stared at him with blank expressions. He flushed red, but when Karen grabbed her cheerleader friends and they started dancing, he rocked as if he really were Stevie Ray Vaughan.

"You aren't doing him any favors," Fay said, as she walked into the backyard where Paul stood beneath the glow of Northern Lights.

"If you could kill him, you would have by now. Tonight I tell him exactly what he is."

Behind them echoed the noise of the party; in the houses

beside Paul's, angry adults watched from closed windows.

"News flash: he knows," Fay said.

"No. He knows your version. I'll tell him whatever will make him my protector." Paul smiled as he turned to face her.

"You arrogant, self-serving, pompous, son of a bitch!"

Fay wanted to tear his throat out and watch him suffer. Luckily for him there were too many witnesses around. Instead she slammed her fist into his face, just as a wolf howled nearby. Paul fell to the ground and someone ran from the house yelling, "All right! A fight!"

Fay stood over Paul and spat, "Jon could have gone home tonight and forgot about all this. He made his choice. I have half a mind to kill you next!"

"There's no contract on me," Paul said smugly.

"You I'd do for the pure pleasure of it," Fay said before returning to the house, ignoring his laughter.

Jon stopped playing and shook out his fingers. The crowd started shouting requests, and Jon wanted to continue, but he knew enough to know that he needed a break.

"I'll play again in fifteen minutes," he told them. His voice cracked, and suddenly he was nervous. Back to being just plain-old Jon. Someone hit play on the stereo, and they started dancing again. Suddenly he went from being the star of the party, right back to being invisible. When he played, all they saw was his music. And when he stopped, he disappeared.

Fay and Karen were nowhere to be seen. Lea was still chatting with Nick. She caught Jon staring and bit her lower lip, then she said something to Nick that made him look over his shoulder and glare at Jon. She started walking towards the stage but stopped, spun back around and returned to Nick. She grabbed his hand and they went upstairs.

Jon just couldn't figure out what her problem was. Then he heard Karen from behind him. "Hi."

"Hi," he replied.

She smiled and handed him a mug. "I thought you might need this."

He hesitated before taking it. Every question he ever had about the After Dusk raced through his mind. He needed to know what she knew, but as she grabbed his hat and put it on, smiling from beneath the wide brim, all he could think was, *You are so hot!*

Karen laughed and gave him back his hat. "I just gave you water. I want you sober enough to keep playing."

Jon reached for the mug, and suddenly the world was in slow motion again. Every other time this had happened Jon's life had been in danger, but what could be dangerous about water? Jon glanced over his shoulder and saw a bottle of beer flying through the air. Inches before it hit his head, he reached out and grabbed it. Then, as the world returned to normal speed, he uncapped the bottle and faced Karen.

"Impressive, young Jedi," she said with a smile.

"Thanks. That first song I wrote myself," he said to her, before taking a swig from the beer. He tried not to gag.

Karen laughed again. "You don't have to drink it to impress me."

Jon considered drinking the beer and pretending to like it. Instead he put it down on a speaker and said, "That's the best news I've had all week."

"Open Arms" played on the stereo, its soft melody bringing couples together on the dance floor. He wanted to ask her to dance, but his confidence had suddenly fled. "Take a walk with me," Karen said.

"Sure," he replied, as she took his hand and led him out of the house.

Lea watched Pyre leave with Karen from a second-story bedroom window. The lights were off in the room and the door clicked as Nick shut it. She couldn't believe that her best friend, the only one she ever really imagined herself dating, had turned into such a stranger. This was about more than just his dead dog.

"Well, we're here," Nick said as he walked up behind her. He put his hands on her shoulders and gave them a squeeze. Here she was alone with Nick, a great guy, yet all she could think about was Pyre.

"Can we just sit and talk?" Lea asked, turning to face him.

He smiled and turned off the bedside lamp. Cast into darkness, Lea could only see a silhouette of Nick as he leaned in and gently kissed her.

"You didn't bring me up here to talk."

"I'm sorry, Nick. I shouldn't have asked you up here. It's not what you probably think." She was blushing, but luckily it was too dark for him to see.

Lea tried to shrug him off, but Nick tightened his grasp. "Nick . . . stop, please!"

"Babe, if you didn't want me then why would you meet me at this party wearing what you're wearing and ask me to the bedroom?"

He threw her to the bed, and when she tried to scramble off the mattress he grabbed her by the chest and pushed her back down. She tried to push him away, but he was far stronger than she was. "Nick! This was a mistake! Please stop!"

He started kissing her again. Lea knew she was in trouble and had to act fast. She could scream for help, or . . . she could slap him hard as she could in the face. Nick recoiled from her palm hitting his cheek.

"What the . . . What was that for?" Nick yelled.

Lea took her chance and scrambled off the bed. "Next time when a girl says no, understand that it means STOP!"

Pyre was right. Nick was a jerk. She stormed out of the room, deciding it was best to go home. She could only hope that Pyre was having an equally rotten time with Karen.

Karen led Jon east down Trout Avenue, past Jack's Hotel to the river. The air was brisk enough for snow but there were no clouds overhead. The Northern Lights streaked pink and green across the sky.

They turned to face each other. Although she still stood a couple inches taller than him, he was no longer as scrawny as he had been. His chest filled out his new jacket, and his arms had the shape of a weightlifter's. Karen brushed her hands over his biceps.

"You've changed considerably since coming to the After Dusk," she said.

"Maybe it was something in the stew," Jon spat.

"So you know then. Jon, listen to me. Whittaker wants

you to figure this out on your own, as if that takes away any of his . . . our . . . wrong-doing. Paul wants to coax you into working for him."

"And you?" Jon asked, stepping back.

"You don't understand. We're being killed, and only you can help us."

Karen's eyes widened and her lower lip trembled as she stared at Jon. No, she was staring past him. She began to tremble all over. "Oh no," she whispered. "He's found me!"

"Karen. You were adopted by the Burrards two years ago," came River's voice.

Jon turned and saw River standing near the Cananee.

Without taking her eyes off River, Karen whispered, "Pyre, run back to the house. Get Fay."

Get Fay? Jon thought, suddenly insulted. He thought about his new powers and said, "I'm not getting Fay! I can take care of this!"

River growled, "Pyre, you are a victim in Whittaker's meddling."

"Minitaw is no longer your hunting ground!"

"I didn't come to Minitaw to hunt vampyres."

"Then why are you killing them?"

"Because they are here!" River shouted. He lifted his head and howled at the moon. His face shifted into the head of a wolf, and steam rose from his clothes. Everything he wore transformed into course fur. River fell on all fours, now a white dire wolf.

Jon stumbled and fell on his back. It was one thing to know what River was, but quite another to see it outside a vision. Nothing could have prepared him for the reality of facing such a terrifying, legendary creature. The wolf leaped towards him – and the world slowed. Jon kicked the beast in the stomach, and it flew backwards. As River rolled, he transformed back into a human and stood up. Jon got back up, scared but unwilling to leave Karen.

She grabbed Jon by the shoulders and whispered in his ears, "We changed you, Pyre. You have the power to stop him. Please!"

"Jon," River said, "you aren't one of them yet. Don't let them turn you."

"I'll save you!" Jon shouted, as he looked back at Karen, just in time to watch her scream as River's fist crossed his temple, knocking him out cold.

CHAPTER EIGHTEEN

October 29th, 1989. Sunday.

J on slowly opened his eyes and looked up at a red sky. He was tired and started to close them again, but when he realized there was someone lightly slapping his cheeks and shouting his name, he forced himself awake. He was lying in the damp mud by the river bank, shivering violently, his clothes soaked. His head throbbed as he focused on Lea, who was kneeling beside him, still in her costume. She looked up and shouted, "Over here!"

The events of the night came back to Jon as he remembered the party, his little concert, his walk with Karen – the punch across his temple that knocked him out cold. But what had happened after that? He didn't have to ask. Lea blubbered, "Karen was attacked by a wolf. When we found her dead, we thought you'd . . ."

Jon saw his parents rush down the river bank.

Lea started crying again and held him tight. His mom, also crying, hugged him, too.

"What happened last night? You got drunk and passed out?" asked his dad.

Jon glared at his dad. "No. I didn't get drunk." He'd never forget what he saw. *River. Werewolf.* Just like the visions.

"I'm okay," Jon said quietly. "Can I just go home?"

"Sure. Come on," his dad said and helped him up. His

mom wouldn't stop fussing, searching to see if he had any cuts or scrapes. She kept saying "tetanus shot" over and over between sobs. Jon ignored it all and walked to the car.

When Jon got home, he went straight to his room and shut the door. The entire trip home his mom had begged that they take him to the hospital, but his dad insisted that Jon was fine. Jon could hear them still arguing about it as he stood in front of his mirror and took off his shirt. Was he fine? Why didn't he have any bruises or cuts or scrapes? If he had gotten hurt, his wounds had healed through the night.

Karen is dead, Jon thought. *She's dead, and I could have stopped it!* If only Whittaker had told him sooner, or Paul had said something, or Fay had been more intent on helping him than killing him. If only he had not been such a wimp and had just accepted these powers for the gift they are. *I could have saved Karen. We could have been together.*

There was a knock on his door. After putting his shirt back on, Jon opened it.

"Can I come in for a second?" his dad asked.

"Sure." Jon collapsed back onto his bed.

"Look, Jon," his dad said, walking to the desk and sitting in the chair. He faced his son, but Jon just stared at the ceiling. "You had a rough night and I don't want to go into punishments. Your mom and I feel like your experience was bad enough, but we can't just ignore the fact that you went to a keg party."

"Dad, please. Not now, okay?"

He sighed. "No, Jon, we're doing this now. Right now. You really scared your mother when she found out this morning that you were missing. Two kids were killed by a wolf, and you're hanging out at the Cananee?"

Jon sat up and said, "Kind of like you hanging out at Sunset Park?"

"Jon, you can't hold that over me to get whatever you want. Do you want to force me into telling your mom?"

"I bet you wish it was me that died."

"I thank God it wasn't, Jon."

"Are you thanking God it was just Karen, then?"

"Jon, would you just listen for a second? I'm trying . . ."

"Trying what? To be a dad? My pal? Don't you usually let mom do the parenting stuff?"

"Right now your mother can't stop crying because she thought she'd lost you!"

Jon whispered, "Thus enters my tearless dad."

Jon stared at his bedspread. His dad got up, the chair squeaking as it spun. "I love you, Jon. If I've given you the impression that I don't, I am truly sorry. I do love you. I just don't get you."

"Yeah, well, I don't exactly get you, either."

"Look, you're grounded until further notice. And unless you want to break up this family, you'll keep your mouth shut."

He didn't wait for Jon to answer. He walked out and shut the door behind him. Jon needed to talk to Whittaker again. But instead he fell back on the bed, too exhausted to do anything but sleep.

The phone rang enough times that the answering machine picked up. Lea sat in her windowsill, listening as the instructions finished, ". . . leave a message at the tone . . ."

"Hey, Lea. It's Nick. Are you there, girl? Pick up."

Did she want to talk to Nick? Definitely not! He had been a real jerk last night, even if his voice did sound ashamed on the machine. How did things get so screwed up?

There was something odd about this "renegade wolf" that seemingly targeted the Whittaker Orphans. Mike, Beverley, Karen . . . and Jon's dog? If it were just a series of random attacks, then this was a Guinness-worthy set of coincidences. But what if it was more? What if these were planned attacks, and poor Cosmo was just in the wrong place at the wrong time?

Outside, the wind blew through the naked trees and rattled the panes of her window. Last night would have been the Halloween Dreams Dance.

Her mom knocked on the door. "Hi, Sweetie. You and I haven't had a chance to talk yet."

"Come in, Mom," Lea said, thankful for the distraction.

She felt as if she were standing on the edge of a cliff ready to fall. Her mom always had a way of fixing that, of bringing her back from the edge into a place of safety. Yet today, her mom had a look in her eyes that was more of a push than a pull.

CHAPTER NINETEEN

he day had started out sunny but now clouds filled the sky. Jon looked out his bedroom window, listening to his parents argue downstairs. *None of this would be happening if only I would stand up to the bullies in my life!* And that's exactly what he was going to do. No more acting like a wimp.

He grabbed the leather jacket and bolero hat that Paul had given him. He put them on and felt a transformation take place. *Jon may have been afraid to stand up to people, but Pyre is stronger!* He started for the door, but didn't want to get into a fight with his father. Not because he was afraid but for his mom's sake. So instead he opened his window, climbed out and jumped to the ground below.

Jon zipped up his jacket as he headed down the highway toward Whittaker's. He had come as far as the junction to Sunset Park when he heard Fay say, "Hey, kid. I thought you might come looking for me."

Jon stared down Devil's Highway and saw her on the bridge. Her bike was parked beside it, packed and ready for her to head out of town. She leaned on the bridge rails, watching the river swirl beneath her.

Jon felt his powers surge through him, just like when he

ate the stew. "River killed Karen."

"*Rancour* has killed a lot of vampyres. Yes, Karen was one of them. But he kills because he thinks all vampyres are evil."

"Did he think Cosmo was evil?"

"I think your dog was just a victim of circumstance."

"Is that what I am?"

Fay leaned against the rails. "Yes."

"And so now you kill me."

"Sorry, kid."

Jon wanted to believe that he could beat her. But he didn't want to kill her, and he knew the only way she'd ever leave him alone is if he did just that. A part of him still didn't believe that she could be a vampyre and that part just couldn't kill. But there was another part of him emerging, one that believed the unbelievable. It was that part of him that had the courage to do what he knew he must: he had to kill her.

Paul came up behind Jon and whispered, "You don't have to die, Jon. Killing an evil vampyre like her isn't wrong."

Jon stared at the rushing river between the bridge rails. Paul continued, "Jon, you want revenge. I can smell it on you. I can help you learn to fight and hunt Rancour. To kill the Wulfsign."

Jon shook his head in disbelief. "By protecting a vampyre."

That's when the world suddenly slowed. Jon turned around and saw a wooden stake flying through the air, fired from a crossbow that Fay wielded. He reached out, grabbed the stake and stopped it from piercing Paul's heart.

"I'm a vampyre, Jon," Paul said, "but even I'm not as fast as you."

Jon ran at Fay and again the air turned thick. Fay's movements seemed slow, easy to block, and when Jon struck her, his strikes were hard and deadly. Fay fell backwards onto the ground, her face cut and her chest heaving. Jon's knuckles were scraped, but they healed almost instantly.

"Jon!" Paul shouted as Fay shot another stake, but this one punctured Paul's heart. He staggered against the rails, bleeding from the wound. When he opened his mouth, blood poured out. He collapsed lifeless to the ground.

"I have to kill you, Pyre!" Fay said, rushing Jon before he had time to react. She punched him in the chest, then sidekicked her heel into his gut. He tried to catch her foot, but she just yanked it back and backfisted him across the ear. His temples rang, and he knew this was the end.

He stood poised to fight. He staggered his feet like he'd seen Bruce Lee do in those late night movies, and when he was in range he threw a punch. Fay laughed and ducked beneath him, slamming her fist into his ribs. He messed up his footing and tripped, landing on the edge of the bridge where he could see the water beneath them.

He remembered the fight he'd had with Nick, right in this very place. Somehow the world had slowed, and he was able to move like a trained fighter. He looked up to see Fay's boot coming down on his head, and rolling away he scrambled to his feet. She spun in a roundhouse kick, but this time Jon willed that the world would slow. Though it happened in choppy moments, like a video stuck between slow motion and regular play, Jon was able to dodge her.

"Say goodbye, Jon," Fay said and reached into her jacket. As she pulled out her pistol, Jon rushed her and grabbed her by the wrist. He twisted her arm so that she dropped the gun, and then he drove his knee up into her stomach. She looked at him with wide, fearful eyes.

"You should have killed me when you had the chance," Jon said as he leaped into the air, feeling weightless, and slammed his foot into Fay's jaw. She stumbled backwards.

"You're not a vampyre. You have no idea how to fight me!" She turned into fog, except for her claws and teeth. She lashed out and caught Jon by surprise, slicing open his chest. He stepped back as she scratched his chest and clawed at his face. He cried out. *How do I fight fog?* Jon grabbed for her, and to his astonishment he could hold onto her fog-form. He punched, and hit her face as if she were corporeal.

With a loud thump Fay landed on the ground, still as fog. "What did Whittaker turn you into?" she whispered.

She rose and attacked, but her movements slowed once again. Jon reached out and grabbed her throat, kicking his knee into her chest. As she doubled over, he drove an elbow into her back so that she fell onto the ground. Turning back to flesh, Fay rolled over and flipped back to her feet. She rushed him, but this time Jon ducked beneath her arms and slammed the stake into her chest. Fay fell back, wide-eyed and open-mouthed. Then she exploded into dust.

CHAPTER TWENTY

"**S**o this is why Pyre's been so cold to me? Because he caught . . ." Lea couldn't say it.

Ms. Black sat on the bed, staring at her feet. "It's over. I promise."

"You're right, Mom. It is over." Lea stood and moved to stand in the doorway. "And I don't just mean the affair."

"Where are you going? We need to talk about this!"

"I'm going out!" Lea shouted and ran downstairs. Grabbing her coat, she slipped into her boots and rushed outside. Her mom didn't follow. As Lea walked the street aimlessly, she started to cry. The cold wind blew at her tears, turning them into frozen sadness.

"This is why I like a natural beauty," Nick said. He'd pulled up beside her, but she hadn't unnoticed due to her warring thoughts.

Lea kept walking and ignored him. Nick parked and hopped out.

"You and I have to talk."

"Nick! Would you just stay away from me?" she said, her voice braver than her beating heart. She looked for the nearest building she could slip into and saw Conway Groceries. She ran to the door, but it was locked. Just then she noticed the "CLOSED" sign.

"We're going for a burger so we can talk about this!" Nick said as he cornered her.

"I'm not hungry," she said.

"Come on, Lea. You're being a bitch."

"Time to say goodbye, Nick," Jon said, as he rode Fay's Honda Shadow up the sidewalk. He got off, and Nick tightened his fists.

"This isn't your business, nerd. Lea and I need to talk and we're going to."

Lea turned to Jon and said, "I can handle this, Pyre."

Jon stopped, dropped the satchel and took off his coat. "This isn't about you, Lea. This is about me and Nick having a score to settle."

Nick took off his coat and smiled. "You think I won't kick your butt in front of her? Come on!"

Lea ran at Nick to stop him from hurting Jon, but Nick pushed her aside, and she fell into the frost-covered grass. Jon didn't move as Nick rushed him. But when Nick grabbed Jon, Jon moved quickly and threw Nick against a tree. The branches at the top shook and snow sprinkled down from them. Nick looked confused.

"Somebody stop them!" Lea screamed.

Nick tried punching Jon, but Jon moved like a pro-boxer. Jon laughed, then hit Nick so hard in the chest that Nick fell to the ground.

Jon kneeled and grabbed Nick by his shirt. He lifted him up and growled, curling his hand back into a fist, "You should have just left me alone!"

Lea ran to Jon and grabbed his arm. "Please, Pyre! Don't!"

When he looked into her eyes, he calmed. Letting go of Nick, he stepped back and stared at his hands. "What did they turn me into?" he whispered.

"Come on, Pyre," Lea said and took his hand. "Let's go."

CHAPTER TWENTY-ONE

ea took him to Icy Shakes, so they would be in a public place. Hopefully, if he was surrounded by people, he would calm down. His eyes darted at different things – the salt and pepper shakers, the ketchup bottle, even the napkin holder. It seemed like he couldn't stay still. "What are you on?" she whispered.

They sat in a small booth opposite each other. It was the only available booth and the restaurant was so busy that it hadn't been cleared yet. Ketchup was smeared over the table and a plate with a half-eaten hamburger and scraps of fries. His gaze settled on the leftover food.

Lea stared at Jon, unsure of what to say. She reminded herself of all the burdens he'd been carrying these last few days. The strange deaths, their parents' affair and the death of poor Cosmo.

"I'm so hungry . . ." Jon said. He looked as if he was struggling not to do something, and then suddenly he started shoveling the leftover food into his mouth. Lea gagged.

"Are you on drugs?" she said finally. "You look crazy."

"Not exactly."

"Pyre, it doesn't matter. What happened back there? You could have killed him. I think you cracked his ribs."

His eyebrows raised. "Do you know what he's done to me?"

"No. Because you never told me. Tell me what's going on." She reached out for his hands, and he held hers tightly.

"You're my best friend, Lea. But I don't think even you would believe me."

Lea sighed. "I will believe you. This is about our parents, isn't it?"

"No, Lea. This is about Mr. Whittaker. About the orphans. And about the wolf attacks. I have to say goodbye to you."

"I don't understand. Are your parents moving?"

Jon held her hand tightly as the waitress came to their table. "Do you want your usuals?" she asked, her lips curling at the sight of the now empty plate of leftover food.

Lea said, "Just a Coke to start."

"Me too," Jon said. When the waitress walked away, he said to Lea, "Have you noticed that I've changed? I'm bigger."

"It's steroids, isn't it? Did Paul sell them to you?"

Suddenly Jon looked into her eyes and said, "I can't tell you this."

They paused as the waitress brought them their drinks.

"You can tell me anything," Lea assured him.

"All I can tell you is goodbye," Jon said, fishing in his pocket for change. "You're the only one who cares enough to come looking for me. Please don't."

Jon tossed a dollar onto the table and headed out. Lea

wanted to rush to him and make him tell her what he was being so cryptic about. But she knew that he was not going to tell her. So she decided to follow him.

Jon walked outside Icy Shakes and listened. He heard nothing. Closing his eyes he concentrated all his energy into his hearing, until there was a loud pop inside his head and every sound hit him all at once: a squirrel cracking a nut, the falling of a leaf . . . the growl from a wolf as it ran beside the Cananee. He ran, faster than any track star, following the sound of the wolf.

The wolf stopped running and within seconds Jon had caught up with it. Right where it had all begun: the After Dusk. He listened again and forced his power back. He heard a struggle inside the bungalow, and he heard someone running towards him from the same direction he'd just come. *Lea! Please don't follow me!*

He couldn't worry about her now. The door hung on its bottom hinge. Inside, Jon heard glass break and wood snap. He grabbed the door, tore it off and stormed inside. Robert lay dead in a corner, a stake in his chest. River, with another stake in his hand, stood over Whittaker. Just as the werewolf brought the stake down, Jon threw the door. It hit River, knocking the stake out of his hand.

"You have chosen to side with the vampyres, then?" River growled.

"You killed Mike. You killed Beverley. You killed Karen. And you killed my dog!" Jon shouted and pointed at River. "I fight for me!"

The werewolf looked at Whittaker and said, "I will kill

you for doing this to a child." Then he turned to Jon. "I will not kill you. But if you stay with these vampyres, I will not give you this same chance when we meet again."

"I won't give you a chance now!" Jon shouted as he lunged at River. The werewolf ducked, narrowly escaping, and slammed his fist into Jon's chest. Jon staggered back but recovered quickly. River kicked low, and Jon leaped. River quickly kicked high, and there was a loud *smack!* as Jon felt the impact of River's foot hitting his chest.

"You can't beat me!" Jon yelled, squaring off as he staggered back a few feet.

"If you fight me, I will kill you," River answered. "I have too much to lose not to."

This time River lashed out and caught Jon in a half-nelson. With his free hand, River punched Jon repeatedly just below the ribs. Jon realized that he wasn't ready to fight the werewolf. Not just yet.

"You will have to kill me to get to Whittaker. Will you kill me the way you did my dog?" Jon managed to squirm around enough to grab River's throat. They struggled, both locked in each other's strong grips.

"No. I won't kill you." River pushed Jon away and shifted into the wolf. Jon squared off again, but the wolf leaped out the window. Jon ran after him, making it to the open pane just in time to see River shift back to a human and get into his Barracuda. The engine roared as the car squealed away.

"You have chosen right. I can train you to fight the werewolf," Whittaker said.

Jon clenched his fists, and the coldness left him. His

powers were getting easier to control he realized, as his heart and senses returned to normal.

"I will be your Defender," Jon said.

"We will leave now. Take nothing with us, so that nothing can be traced back to us. We will create new identities and new lives. Start the After Dusk over again," Whittaker said to Jon. They left through the back door where a van was parked outside. Whittaker took the driver's seat, but before Jon got in he heard Lea yell, "Pyre!"

Jon turned to face her. She stood where she could see inside the broken door, and he knew that she had witnessed everything. Jon wished he could take away what she'd just seen. Now she knew what he had become. *What I have willingly become.*

"Lea, I told you not to follow me!"

She took a few steps towards him, then stumbled backwards as if she considered running away. Her mouth stayed poised as if ready to scream.

"Goodbye," he whispered. He stayed still for a second, watching her tremble, watching the tears stream down her cheeks. "Don't search for me."

She shook her head. "I . . . I won't."

"Pyre!" Whittaker yelled.

Jon turned and walked to the van. He recalled what he'd seen in Whittaker's vision, when River had said, *"A vampyre killed my soul-mate. I hunt him and any other whose path I cross!"* He glared at Whittaker and growled, "Rancour won't follow us. We were just in his way. Once we're gone, the murders will stop."

Jon climbed into the passenger seat and they drove off.

"I've given up everything, Whittaker," he said, watching Lea in his side view mirror until she disappeared from sight. "One day you'd better deliver Rancour to me."

"Once you are trained and ready to defeat him, I promise that I will."

November 16, 1998.

Vampyres are a disease and must be erased. Yet I do more than act like a cure. I am an executioner, for the disease and for the sin that surrounds it.

When I hunt, I send a message. One that has earned me the most feared reputation in all the vampyre community. My message is simple: reform or die.

A reputation that is known as Pyre.

But no matter how many I stake, they are all just practice for the next time I meet Rancour the Wulfsign. For he is the disease I will spend my life fighting to eradicate.

JAMES McCANN *survived cancer at a very young age.*
He currently works as a children's book specialist
and teaches creative writing workshops for teens,
using mapmaking as the basis of his methodology.
He is also the author of Rancour
and Upon the Shoulders of Vengeance.
James McCann lives in Vancouver, B.C.
with his Shih Tsu, Conan.

———